to swing his sword for some rich chick's birthday party, he goes along as a favor. Then he spies sweet Annaliese watching his moves and knows she's the one.

A LEAP YEAR LOVE TRIANGLE ... *can they make it last?*

When Jack sees the way Annaliese looks at Ransom, he's ready to back away ... until Ransom invites him to a private after-party for three. Can Annaliese overcome her shyness to share passion with not one, but two hot men?

Warning: This story contains hot ménage and demonstrations of affection between two alpha heroes and one heroine.

I0545248

From *Surprise for Three: Leap Year*

When the white-haired woman signaled the DJ to aim a spotlight at the tiered cake, Annaliese's hopes plummeted. The confection was covered in red roses and sugar hearts. Pretty, not sexy.

Her eyes stung with tears. Not a bang, not a whimper, but an awww. Oh Ransom, I tried.

Then the older woman heaved off the top three layers of the cake—the real birthday cake for eating later—and set it on a nearby table. It left the covered cart plus a cardboard cake base, the two together just high enough for a person to crouch inside.

Annaliese's hopes returned with a rushed inhale. Was there at least a sexy exotic dancer inside?

Especially, was she sexy enough to wow Ransom?

The grandmotherly woman mounted the platform and took over the mic.

"Ladies and gentlemen." Her alto rang like a showmaster's. "Please sing a rousing 'Happy Birthday' to—" she checked the slip of paper Annaliese had given the DJ, and her eyes opened in shock, but she was already shouting, "—Ransom!"

The fake tiers and cart burst in half. A tanned body stepped from inside.

"Surprise!"

The body was big, hard and muscled. Gorgeous, yes. That body could fell a horse.

Annaliese stared, not in surprise, but shock.

The stripper was a man.

Surprise for Three: Leap Year

Will she dare to take a leap this bold?

Part of the Leap Year collection

THE GIRL NEXT DOOR ... *she's not daring enough for him*

Annaliese loves Ransom, but has given up on winning his heart. It hurts too much to watch him with other women, so she's leaving town. In farewell, she throws him a Leap Year birthday party—with a surprise. She may not get his heart a-pumping, but the beautiful exotic dancer popping out of the cake will.

THE RICH PLAYBOY ... *he's too much of a risk-taker for her*

Ransom's heart belongs to Annaliese, but he's convinced he'd make her miserable, since he craves the adrenaline rush of extreme sports and kinky sex. He can only hope his passion for her matures before another man sweeps her away ... and then the giant cake is wheeled in.

THE WOUNDED WARRIOR ... *she's just what he's looking for*

Jack is home from duty as a Navy SEAL and on the hunt for a sweet woman to settle down with. When a relative maneuvers him into a pirate costume

Look for these titles
by Remi Bond

Now Available:

Surprise for Three

Surprise for Three

Leap Year

Remi Bond

Surprise for Three
Copyright © 2016 by Mary Hughes
Digital ISBN: 978-1-940958-09-5
Print ISBN: 978-1-940958-10-1
Cover by P and N Graphics

First electronic publication: March 2016
First print publication: March 2016

DEDICATION

My profound thanks to the dedicated men and women serving in our nation's armed forces. Their training and commitment is an inspiration.

Taking the Leap this Year with S.L. Carpenter, fun, smart, and so talented everything he does is covered with genius sauce.

Huge thanks to S.L. Carpenter and P and N Graphics for the genius cover, and to The Blurb Queen for sharpening the blurb to a royally fine point.

To Gregg, as they all are.

Chapter One

"What do you mean, the cake was scheduled for *yesterday?*" Annaliese pressed her cell phone to her tightening jaw. "I need it *today,* at seven o'clock sharp."

She flipped her phone for a quick check of the time—already nearly five. This was a party planner's nightmare. She clapped the phone to her ear.

"My sincere apologies." The grandmotherly tone on the other end was pitched at soothing. "The clerk heard 'last day of February' and scheduled you for the twenty-eighth."

Annaliese nearly ground down her molars. The whole point of this Leap Year birthday party was today's rare February twenty-ninth. She shuddered to think what would have happened if she hadn't done her usual event-day triple check.

A party without a cake? Unthinkable. Especially this party and this cake.

"Look—Lilly, was it? Lilly, I ordered the Deluxe Pop-out. Will you be able to fulfill my request or do I have to go somewhere else?"

"Sweet Treats always satisfies, ma'am. The cake is still fresh. I'll get it and the cart now."

"And the pop-out?" Annaliese lowered her voice. "I asked for your most—exotic—dancer." Meaning most beautiful.

"Yes ma'am. Don't worry, we have exactly what you need." The woman hung up.

Smashing a finger against call-end, Annaliese took a deep breath and consciously relaxed her jaw. Problem handled—hopefully. Normally she didn't let little hitches bother her. They were part of the job.

Tonight is more than just a job, isn't it? She called up her event to-do list, phone stylus poised over the cake checkbox. If this had been merely another event, she'd have been satisfied with perfect.

For Ransom, for saying goodbye to him and her dreams, tonight had to be better than perfect.

Skipping the cake, she went on down the list. Champagne fountain, check. Royal purple streamers, paper lanterns, and table favors, check. Buffet tables, check. Catering vans parked in the rear parking lot of Ransom's huge home, check. Caterers bearing food like an ant-line from the service entrance, setting up shrimp and aged cheeses and finger éclairs. Check.

She stepped back and smiled. Lovely.

Then the birthday boy glided into the room—or rather, birthday *man.*

Ransom's six-foot-two frame, his swimmer's physique enhanced by a hand-tailored suit, showed off the fact that he was all deliciously grown up.

Her body quivered in reaction, heart beating faster at the sight of him, as it always did. *Maybe I could stay in town...?*

Damn it, no. To Ransom, she would never be more than a friend. He needed more than she could give, and she wanted more than *he* could give. So she'd accepted a new position, an alumni relations gig, in a city as far away from him as she could get.

Telling him tonight. Her stomach clenched at the thought. *After the cake.*

He stalked through the festive room like a lion through pansies, making every decoration, every fun touch she had painstakingly selected, look a little ridiculous. She sighed.

Just by being Ransom, he turned her world on its head, as he had from the beginning.

"Annie!" He spotted her, sapphire eyes lighting, turning his already handsome face into insanely gorgeous.

Her bare arms rumpled with goose bumps, and her thighs clenched with a bright splash of need beneath the swingy skirt of her dress. *Double damn it.*

He arrowed toward her, his long-legged stride covering the distance between them as fast as a jet, cutting through the ballroom-size living room, owning the space, dominating it. Ransom needed two things—a challenge and room to soar.

They were the most unlikely of friends. But friends they were.

"Thanks so much for this party." He seized her upper arms in his strong hands and pulled her in for a kiss—to the cheek.

Not nearly the kiss she wanted, but even the light buss made her belly tremble. Every time he touched her, the feel of his lips on her skin, the heat of his breath, made her forget that they were only friends.

Made her yearn for things he wasn't offering.

She loved him. She burned for an intimate relationship with him, the twining of bodies, hearts, and souls.

Though she'd settle for some pounding red-hot sex. *Face it. You want anything you can get from him.*

Triple damn it. If only she were a supermodel or rich debutante instead of the girl next door.

But she was only sweet little Annie to him. Remembering that, she pulled back.

He released her, smiling down at her. "This is amazing. A real blow-out job."

She blinked. That sounded like code for sex. Although, with Ransom, with how she felt about him, everything sounded like code for sex to her. "I do my best."

"Well, it's spectacular, and I thank you. But I do worry you work too hard, Annaliese. You didn't have to do all this, you know. It's just a birthday."

"You're kidding, right?" She couldn't ignore *this* birthday. Ransom was a leap year baby, and his actual birthday came only once every four years, so she was determined to give him a bash he'd remember—and remember her by—forever. "I appreciate your concern, Ransom, but this is what I do. I organize. Now shoo. I have work to do." She turned to her clipboard app and checked off the second-last item, chocolate fountain, pretending to ignore the heat of his big body touching hers.

One checkbox remained virgin. The big finale, the goodbye to her dreams.

The birthday cake.

Ransom craved excitement almost like a junkie. He needed that adrenaline rush. So her last gift to him, before she walked away forever, was the Sweet Treats deluxe cake—and the stripper who'd pop out of it.

Because if a sexy exotic dancer didn't get Ransom's adrenaline going, nothing would.

At first she'd shared his love of the excitement. Her heart beat faster, remembering how he'd pedaled her away on her first grand adventure, a sweet-smelling farmer's field where she picked wildflowers and ate stolen strawberries. They were estate manager's daughter versus estate heir, but Ransom never let his cash stand in the way of their friendship.

It was his taste for wild entertainment that moved him out of her emotional reach. Her heart stuttered. With her pretty, not exotic, face and figure, her nature to plan parties, not wild nights, he needed more than she could give. Still, she wanted him to be happy.

"Hey, punkin'. What's wrong?" His strong, warm finger slid under her chin, tipping her face toward him.

She resisted, staring at the virgin check mark, watery in her sight. She loved him, knew what he needed, and was by-damn going to give it to him.

Even if it was never *her* popping out of his cake.

"What could be wrong? I'm throwing you the birthday party to beat all birthday parties." She let him raise her gaze to his, willing a smile all the way to her eyes. "You love that, right?"

"Annie..." He studied her intently, slowly shaking his head. "I know you. Tell me what's bothering you."

Damn. She hadn't fooled him. She never could, not when he really looked. He did care about her, just not the way she needed—which made it even more painful.

She waved a hand at his mansion's huge living room, done over for the party. "I'm just worried everything goes off okay."

"It will." A faint smile curved his lips. "You're planning it. You're the best, Annaliese."

"The best," she echoed faintly. *Not true. If I were the best, I'd be the woman spiking Ransom's adrenaline.*

The best woman would excite his dreams, his blood, and his bed.

Annaliese's heart broke that it wasn't her.

*   *   *

"Jack, wait up a moment."

The motherly alto stopped Jack in his silent pad across the office. Business manager Lilly, not even looking up from her paperwork, waved him toward her overflowing desk. *How does she know I'm here?* He'd moved soundlessly from habit. Had she detected his scent or were there webcams—? Not that he hadn't already checked. Whatever it was, it'd make her a mint as a covert operative.

He could've used it six months ago, when a bullet nearly bought him a voyage home in a wooden box.

Lilly ran Sweet Treats, the innocuous name of a party service that featured exotic dancers for shindigs from bachelor to birthday—specialty, jumping out of a cake.

Now she glared at her computer screen as if she'd set it on fire.

"What's wrong?" Jack turned in the doorway, glad *he* wasn't her monitor.

"Treanie made a huge mistake." She shook her head, white bun shivering. "Honestly, if she weren't my niece's daughter, I'd suggest she switch careers. Maybe take up blowing up balloons. The woman breathes helium."

"Details aren't her strong point," Jack said mildly.

Lilly grinned, still at the monitor, but her smile faded almost immediately. Then she looked up over her glasses.

The blue of her irises, underlined by dark tortoise shell, hit him like twin lasers. He flinched.

Big military special ops that he was, even he cringed when she used that look. "What." His word was more dread than question.

"Jack, I need you to step in."

He groaned. He worked maintenance at Sweet Treats because Lilly was his mother's sister's cousin's...something. Aunt, or mother-in-law, or congressional rep for all he knew. His mother kept track of those things, down to the once- and twice-removed. All he knew was that he and Lilly were relatives, and when he was going stir-crazy from his injury and needed to get out of the house—or rather, his mother needed him out from under her feet—Lilly just happened to have a job.

Hell, all he'd been trying to do was help his mother with the tidying. What was wrong with giving your mother a hand? Just because she didn't like him dusting with industrial canned air...

"Now, don't you start giving me that black-thundercloud look," Lilly said. "Doesn't scare me none."

"I wasn't scowling at you." He waved a hand at the door. "I *was* about to leave for the day—"

"Jack, Treanie really screwed the pooch this time."

"Sorry to hear that. But—"

"She's related to you too, you know."

Of *course* she was. "All right, what'd she do?"

"Not only did she get the date wrong, but there's this. It's a fiasco." She twisted her monitor toward him and thunked a finger against the screen. "The request is for a Deluxe Pop-out Cake with a female dancer."

"So?"

"*So*," she jabbed at the screen, "the *client* is a woman. I just spoke with her. Ninety-nine times out of a hundred, a woman requesting a stripper means a gal party, a bachelorette or birthday. They need a *male* dancer."

"So get one of the men on the roster." When she continued to stare he felt forced to defend himself with, "I handle odd jobs—"

"This *is* an odd job." One gray brow rose.

Her hair was white but her brows weren't merely gray, they were iron gray. Gun-metal gray. Bullet-between-the-eyes gray.

Jack held up both palms. "Non-naked-getting odd jobs."

"You don't have to get naked." She twisted the monitor back to her and, eyes dropping to the screen, began to type. "G-string is fine."

"I'm not—"

"The job is in less than two hours, and the drive will take at least half that. Every man I've called is busy or not answering his phone. You're it. D'you think I'd ask if it weren't an emergency? Please? Just this once, Jack. I need a man, and I need him *now*."

Jack felt like he was floundering. "I'm a man, but—"

"Great!" She tapped a keyboard key. Behind her, a printer hummed, warming up. "Here's everything you need to know. Costumes are in back."

"I know where the costumes are." After he'd fixed one of the clothing racks, he'd entertained himself for half an hour rummaging through the outfits. Sweet Treats racked everything from French Maid to Dungeon Master. "But I'm not. I can't." He made a final appeal. "I don't know how to dance."

"Except for the year you took in first grade, courtesy of the Rec Department." The printer chunked out a page.

"How did you—oh. Mom?"

"Yes. But I've got eyes, haven't I? Your body's made for dancing." She grabbed the paper and held it toward him. "Try it, you might like it."

What I'd like, *now that I'm* former *active duty and permanently home from the front line, is to find a nice girl and settle down.* But he only eyed the paper without taking it. "I'm perfectly happy doing my usual job of fixing stuff then going home. I'd really rather you find someone else."

"Jack, please. Sweet Treats' reputation is on the line. My reputation as office manager is on the line. Our family's reputation is on the line. There *is no one else*. I need you to fill in. *Please?*" Somehow Lilly managed, by tilting her head or pursing her lips or some matronly trick, to make her blue eyes shimmer through her thick glasses lenses, as if with tears.

Damn, was her lower lips trembling?

"Fine." He snatched the paper from her. "But only this once."

"Thanks. I owe you."

Her relieved smile was almost worth the pain he was going to endure. Him, dance? He'd be like an M16 assault rifle waving its butt.

As he headed for the costume room, she called out, "By the way, you should wear the pirate costume. It's naughty but not too revealing—and best of all, your size."

He didn't bother asking how she knew what size he wore.

*　　*　　*

Ransom stood—not running, jumping, flying, but standing tediously *still*—near the door, where Annaliese had stationed him, saddled as the birthday boy with welcoming duty. In the background a DJ played standard pop music. The tune might be pumping out at two pulses a second, but his heart rate was a boring fifty-four beats per minute.

"Hello." The purr came from yet another gorgeous woman, the latest in an unending line, a blonde swiveling in on admittedly sexy blue-sequined high heels.

"Welcome." He pasted on a smile and dutifully admired her lycra-and-silicone engineering. Normally he enjoyed the mild zing flirting gave him, but tonight he was bored out of his mind.

Standing there. His heart rate a staid fifty-four bpm.

Then the familiar scent of honey and cinnamon wafted in the air, spiking his heart rate double as Annaliese flit past, putting invisible touches on an already-perfect buffet. Invisible touches to him, at any rate. The moment she left the table, a cloud of guests descended on that spread like locusts.

She left his sight and her scent left his nose, and his heart rate returned to the staid waltz tempo.

"Nice party." The blonde clutched her purse to her breasts in a not-so-subtle move to plump her already impressive cleavage.

Lub-dub, lub-dub... He sighed. "My friend put it together for me."

As he chatted with the blonde, Annaliese again flit into view, to correct the next minutely imperfect thing. He was grateful to her for this birthday party, truly he was, but he wished she'd stop working and enjoy.

"Must be a good friend.

"My *best* friend." He loved Annaliese. Had for years. He'd probably marry her some day—when he was older and slower and wiser.

When all the mountains had been climbed and skies had been flown and he could settle down to be the man she wanted. Maybe even the man she needed.

"He sounds wonderful," the blonde said.

He, right. The reminder that Annaliese might find someone else before Ransom was ready to settle down gave him a twinge of indigestion. He smiled through it. If she found a man who brought her joy, that would be great, right? He only wanted her to be happy.

Which was why he hadn't proposed already—Ransom knew he'd make her miserable.

His stomach turned sour. Before he took his indigestion out on the blonde, he suggested, "Why don't you get some shrimp, before they're all gone?"

"Oh. Right." The blonde swiveled away.

A white lie. Annaliese would never let the food run out at a bash she'd organized.

"Hi." Almost immediately another gorgeous woman, this one a brunette in a glittery red dress, came to replace—he couldn't remember the first's name. Ms. Blue Sequins.

"Welcome." He wanted Annaliese to be happy, but he made her miserable. Like the time he'd finally talked her into sky diving. She was white and vomiting before the plane even took off. Thinking she only needed an example to see how fun and perfectly safe it was, he leaped out first.

He'd dropped through the sky alone. Landed alone.

"Nice party."

"Thanks. My friend—my best friend—threw it for me." He'd tried to ease Annie into his lifestyle, but with each parasailing or whitewater rafting or bungee jump, she got more and more withdrawn.

Which hurt him too. He'd only wanted to share with her the exhilaration, the sheer joy of being alive.

Finally he'd put a stop to her suffering, and stopped asking.

It had nearly killed him.

Annaliese glanced up at that moment. Her gaze landed directly on him, as if she'd sensed his pain.

Attuned to him, *with* him, as she always was. His pain eased.

Damn it, she'd gone to a great deal of trouble to make today perfect for him—even though he'd rather she have fun than he have perfection—and it would be rude of him not to at least try to enjoy himself. He smiled at her.

She smiled back and returned to adjusting some unseen flaw in her preparations.

"Is your friend here?" Ms. Red Glitter asked brightly.

Yes. She's here working, instead of standing in line with me as my hostess, because if I married her, I'd break her heart.

He'd never even had sex with her. At first he thought it was because he cherished their friendship and didn't want to ruin that with disappointing vanilla intercourse.

But then he realized the problem was him. He was the one who craved the thrill of the chase, the excitement of variety. He was the one who couldn't settle down.

What was wrong with him? Why couldn't he bed the woman he loved, instead of a parade of women whose names he couldn't remember?

"I said, your friend," the woman repeated. "Is he here?"

A flash of anger, at how unfair life was but mostly at himself, made him snap, "Yes, *she* is."

"Oh." The syllable dripped frost. "Well, enjoy."

He sighed as red-spangled hips twitched off and the next gorgeous woman took their place, seductively curved lips the exact pink of her tube dress. Interchangeable as ice cubes. His heart rate slowed almost as if the organ had been dipped in ice water.

He wondered when even sex had left him so bored and jaded.

The squeal of cart wheels in need of oil caught his attention. His heart paused in its comfortable lub-dub.

Back of the room, coming through the service entrance. He turned toward the noise.

A matronly woman pushed a cart bearing a huge cake.

Ransom's heart kicked back in, pace picking up. A *surprise*. Stripper, probably, but if Annaliese picked the company, the stripper would be first-class. He found himself, for the first time, intrigued.

Chapter Two

Despite scurrying around with last-minute adjustments, Annaliese heard the instant the cake came squeak-squeaking in. Relief flooded her, snapping almost immediately to panic. She'd wanted to see Ransom's face as the cake entered, to judge his reaction. She spun toward the door and immediately saw him.

Interest lit his eyes.

Yes. She gave a mental fist-pump of triumph. She'd done it. She'd finally excited her adrenaline junkie.

She only hoped the woman inside the cake would measure up to Ransom's standards. He dated supermodels and daughters of the rich and pampered. Only the best would do for him. Wondering if she could judge the woman inside the cake by the person outside, she checked the figure pushing the cart.

Her chest froze. A grandmotherly woman trundled the cake into place before the DJ's stage.

Had Sweet Treats gotten the order wrong? Was this simply a regular cake, and Annaliese was going out with a whimper instead of a bang? Her hopes belly flopped, splat, into her stomach.

When the white-haired woman signaled the DJ to aim a spotlight at the tiered cake, Annaliese's hopes plummeted. The confection was covered in red roses and sugar hearts. Pretty, not sexy.

Her eyes stung with tears. Not a bang, not a whimper, but an *awww*. *Oh Ransom, I tried.*

Then the older woman heaved off the top three layers of the cake—the real birthday cake for eating later—and set it on a nearby table. It left the covered cart plus a cardboard cake base, the two together just high enough for a person to crouch inside.

Annaliese's hopes returned with a rushed inhale. Was there at least a sexy exotic dancer inside?

Especially, was she sexy enough to wow Ransom?

The grandmotherly woman mounted the platform and took over the mic.

"Ladies and gentlemen." Her alto rang like a showmaster's. "Please sing a rousing 'Happy Birthday' to—" she checked the slip of paper Annaliese had given the DJ, and her eyes opened in shock, but she was already shouting, "—Ransom!"

The DJ dropped the needle on the traditional song. Party goers happy on champagne sang an enthusiastic, if not quite tuneful, rendition of the words. This could still go well. If the dancer inside the cake was gorgeous, everything Annaliese hoped for...

The fake tiers and cart burst in half. A tanned body stepped from inside.

"*Surprise!*"

The body was big, hard and muscled. Gorgeous, yes. That body could fell a horse.

Annaliese stared, not in surprise, but shock.

The stripper was a man.

*   *   *

Half-blind, Jack stared at the sea of faces. Damned pirate's patch. Lilly's scowl meant he couldn't *not* wear the damned thing, but he'd been careful to place it over his non-trigger eye.

Blank faces stared back at him like a wall of stones. He thought about getting stage fright.

Then the heavy beat music started. Lilly hissed, "Dance."

Yeah. A SEAL never worried about stage fright, he got the job done. Besides, Lilly needed him to do this. So he'd do this.

He strode into the heart of the spotlight and shouted, "Avast ye birthday partiers. Here be treasure!" He tore off the pirate hat and sent it sailing into the crowd.

Arms shot up, hands grabbing for the tricornered felt as if it were a wedding bouquet. Several feminine fingers landed on it at the same time.

That hat was gone for good.

Behind him, Lilly sighed loudly. He ignored her. He knew she'd figured some costume loss into the fee.

Assuming he could earn it by actually dancing.

He'd chewed on that all the way here. Yes, he'd had a year of Rec Department dancing, but beginner tap-and-ballet wouldn't be what Lilly had in mind. For a group of partying women, the more raucous and horny-making, the better.

What *would* impress them, at least from his experience dating, was seeing his body. While to him, the muscles roping his arms, chest and legs were simply useful, to women it represented the power he'd bring to lovemaking.

So. He'd dance like he'd make love.

Start slow, easy. Twisting his shoulders, he flexed forearms and biceps bared by the pirate costume's sleeveless vest.

Appreciative murmurs greeted him. *Doin' it right, then.*

A few more pumps of arm and chest muscles got more ahhs, and a short groan or two. *Time to step up the tempo.* He twirled off the vest, revealing his obliques. Gasps and a few oohs greeted that.

He hid a grin. Okay, he could do this. He could earn Lilly her fee and not embarrass himself too badly.

He spun the vest around one finger and tossed it—behind him, so Lilly wouldn't have a fit.

As he pumped a few more muscles on his now-naked torso, individual faces began to resolve in the crowd. He wasn't sure if the light was getting better, his eye was adjusting, or his adrenaline rush was wearing off. He started to see individuals, their curved lips, sparkling eyes, and cheeks glowing with admiration.

This was almost fun.

He swung a couple experimental dance moves, a grapevine and kick-ball-change, ending with a quick spin.

Cheers, louder for each, egged him on. On the way here, he'd told himself he'd only strip off the vest, then dance their hearts away. But the enthusiastic shouts tempted him to go further; the bright faces urged him to take off more.

Ah, what the hell. The leather chaps, made to look like pants, fastened with a rip-strip. He tore them off with one good yank, leaving him clad in a g-string, sword belt, boots, and the eye patch.

His nipples and bare flesh puckered in the sudden cold—until the delighted claps and shrieks of women in the crowd seemed to clothe him again, caressing him like velvet.

Their excitement and the moment carried him, giving him the confidence to try a bump and grind.

Hoots and good-natured catcalls greeted his move, seemingly light, but his training made him ultra-aware of every nuance in his environment. He heard how the female voices darkened with arousal.

His cock stirred in its pouch, knowing it was now the center of attention, and appreciative attention at that.

Dance like he'd make love? Copy that.

Fisting his hands in the air, he began to roll his hips, rocking a rhythm as old as time, slow and easy at first.

Faces flushed before him. One or two sets of nipples pinpointed tight dresses. The room definitely turned hotter, the satiny musk of arousal dusting the air. The shrieks died down to low, barely heard groans as he rolled his abs like a coaster-ride. In the crowd, tongues licked ruby lips and hips moved almost unconsciously, as if he were making love to each of them.

He turned sideways and strutted before the stage, arms closing around an imaginary partner, hips thrusting faster. Harder. He turned the other way, going faster still.

He turned toward the crowd, lifted his arms, put his hands behind his head, and drove into it with everything he had.

Mid-thrust, his gaze collided with the most beautiful gingerbread-brown eyes in the world.

Time froze, his breath with it.

A sweet face went along with the eyes. Kind. Loving. The kind of face he'd imagined to get through repeated tours of duty.

The kind of face he'd dreamed of waking up to one day.

His cock burst with shock, inflating like a lifeboat, nearly tearing from the pouch.

It's her. She's the one.

*　　*　　*

When the cart rolled in, Ransom was mildly interested. When a guy instead of a gal shot from the cake, his heart rate jumped to an excited hundred bpm. But then seeing the guy's hard body, his rolling hips...well, if the pirate's sexual technique was as good as his dancing, he'd have women all around on their backs, panting, with their legs spread.

Then the pirate tore off his chaps and started thrusting and that *erection*, holy shit.

Ransom pressed a hand to his chest. His heart hammered beneath his palm.

It suddenly occurred to him, if the guy was this arousing to another guy, how would he be to Annaliese? Yeah, she was laced pretty tight, but she *was* female.

He closed his eyes and let his internal sense find her. Somehow, he always knew where she was. He didn't think it was mystical, just a friend thing. *There.* He turned, opened his eyes and saw her, a little ways ahead of him but edging toward the front of the crowd pressing around the pirate, almost as if she couldn't help herself. He hurried after her.

From her gaping jaw, she was as stunned by the guy as he was. He swallowed a smile. Probably she'd ordered the usual cheesecake and got beefcake instead, her perfect planning overturned by random acts of chaos. Yeah, life was messy.

Messy meant *exciting*.

Maybe she'd feel that now. Maybe she'd *enjoy* that now. Heart thumping even harder, Ransom eased himself into her wake, moving closer to see her better. Oh *yeah*.

She wasn't simply gaping. Her nostrils flared and her face was flushed. Her wet tongue peeked out as if it wanted to flirt with the pirate's buried treasure.

She was *aroused*.

A hot flare of delight astonished Ransom—and *singed* him. He loved the adrenaline rush, but seeing *Annaliese* enjoying one sent him flying.

Her eyes dropped to the pirate's hips. The exotic dancer was showing off his muscles with sensual thrusts of his pelvis. A low moan ripped from her throat, nearly drowned by the groans of the women in the crowd, but Ransom was attuned to every shading of her voice.

The guy's swinging pirate sword got her all hot and bothered? *Hell, yeah*.

Her eyes rose as the dancer turned front, driving hips into his audience like a freight train—and he froze.

His dark, one-eyed gaze locked on Annaliese.

She stared back, shocked.

Ransom could almost see the bolt of electricity between them.

Jealousy ripped through him. Annaliese was *his*. His friend, the one who was always there for *him*...

Damn it Ransom, get a grip. Hadn't he just been thinking that if she found someone who brought her joy, he'd be happy for her?

So why wasn't he delirious now?

Chapter Three

As the dancer's hips rippled, thrusting his sizeable pouch into stark relief, Annaliese was so turned on she could barely breath. The man was seriously built. He had muscles and, from the battle scars on his big, dangerous body, they weren't just for show. Watching him dance, he not only knew how to use his brawn, he had the power and strength to use it to the hilt.

Hilt. Shuddering, she tried not to think what that pouch would feel like, grinding between her slick thighs, driving a thick erection into her, *to the hilt.*

Grinding, pumping, thrusting, *hard...*

Oh heavens. *Not* thinking of it only made it crystal clear.

She squirmed, trying to adjust her stance to cool her rapidly dampening crotch. *Look at his face. That'll help me cool down...* She looked up, precisely as the pirate stripper turned front with a driving thrust *to the hilt—*

Looking directly at her.

She stopped breathing. Tried to swallow. Stuck. He had the most amazing dark gaze...

*   *   *

Jack's gaze locked with the woman, who had somehow become bathed in a halo of golden light.

Cinnamon hair, gingerbread eyes, lips like cherries... She looked so sweet he could eat her up. And somewhere, deep inside, he decided if she'd let him, he would.

His head started spinning. Fuck, he wasn't breathing. His training had deserted him and left him in this schoolboy state. Open to enemy sniper or mortar or any damned thing...

The woman blushed and glanced down.

He'd *scared* her? His breath returned in sucked alarm. His hearing returned too. His heart beat in his ears, too loud and too fast, like a double drum line—punctuated by a strange hiss.

"*Psst*." The hiss boiled into words. "Mr. Woody's escaping." Lilly, reminding him he had an audience.

Hell. He glanced down, saw he had an erection that could be marked from space. One more inch and the thing would go from peeking to waving *hi-how-ya-doin'?* No wonder the angel had looked away. The moment he thought of the cinnamon-haired woman, his dick went from pirate-size R to XXX. Without his hat to cover himself, he had few options.

Dropping to the floor, he started doing alternating one-armed push ups.

More cheers, so that was okay.

While he pumped, he thought furiously. What did he do now, besides the times tables, to will down his wood? He wanted the woman. Wanted to touch her, kiss her, *pound into her until they were both breathless*...but he'd probably better start with asking her on a date.

Problem—though he'd met women in bars and even had some of Lilly's dancers offer him a night or two, he hadn't asked a women for a date in years.

He switched arms and pumped out a few double-time. Fuck. Tours of duty were easy compared to this. In a combat situation, all he had to do was whatever it took to achieve the mission objectives.

Switch, up, down. What if he did that now? Okay. Mission—sweep that sugar-sweet-looking woman off her feet. First objective, meet her. Strategy, finish this damned dance, then go after her. Say hi, then...then what? Some subtle approach...

He glanced up. She was watching him again, her eyes on him glowing like amber rock-candy crystals, her lips parted as if she was having trouble breathing.

Okay, maybe his approach wouldn't have to be too subtle.

Then, as he bobbed up and down, catching snapshots of her between the standing bodies, he saw her gaze shift.

Turning. Looking beside her.

At a *man.*

Blood firing, Jack glimpsed details as he seesawed up and down. Thirties. Fit body. Clothes tailored, so rich. Blond, but that manly type with dark eyebrows and a stubble along his honed jaw. Narrow, aristocratic nose.

Too fucking handsome for Jack's taste, but the woman smiled at the blond.

A growl burned Jack's belly. Up-down, up-down...his arms would start to burn soon too, but his brain was already blazing. From the way she was looking at the guy, with a pleading little smile, he was someone special to her.

And one thing more—from the heat steaming her gaze, she wanted him.

Jack changed hands, slamming his fist into the floor. He wanted to smash a five-finger salute into the rich guy's face.

Until he saw his angel's lips close—she wasn't having trouble breathing with Mr. Blondie.

Yeah, well, she may think she wants him, but only until I rock her world.

Same mission, charm her into a date. Same first objective, meet her. Anger had boiled the blood out of his erection so he leaped to his feet. New strategy, finish this damned dance then surmount all obstacles—including her attraction to Mr. Richass—however he had to, and go after her.

Then the blond man's gaze turned to *Jack,* and it was shrewd and assessing. A light entered the blond's eye. A crafty light.

Jack's blood fritzed like a thousand bee stings. With intuition born of hundreds of deadly situations, he knew he was in deep shit.

*   *   *

Ransom met Annaliese's pleading gaze and understood immediately that she didn't know what she was asking for—she didn't even know she was asking.

But he did. He'd seen the entire rainbow of her moods—happy, angry, sad, and though he'd never seen the golden glow to her before, he knew instinctively what it was.

Searing physical attraction.

She was totally aroused, her nipples poking against the knit of her dress, her mouth moist from licking, her hips rocking as if she couldn't stand still.

The *pirate* had done that to her.

Her gaze returned to the muscular man, her irises brightened to golden sands around dilated pools of black. In all the years Ransom had known her, she'd never looked at any other man this way. Not even him.

The bile of jealousy left an acrid tang in his mouth.

He immediately scolded himself. She deserved better from him.

He swallowed his envy and dug down deep inside to find his best self, the man who was first Annaliese's friend.

I have to be her wingman. It's unfamiliar territory, but I can do it for Annaliese, right?

Okay. The way she looked at the guy, she needed to have sex with him or she'd burst.

On the other hand, this was Annaliese. She wasn't a bang 'em and buh-bye 'em kind of woman. She talked a lot about romance, about a one-and-only relationship. *She'd* never go after the pirate simply to see what all the fuss was about, or even just to get her rocks off.

But if she didn't go after the guy, what would happen once he danced out of her life? Would she be forever scarred by *what-if?*

No, it was obvious to Ransom that *he'd* have to get them together. Based on the electricity in their gazes, if he could maneuver them into the same room, lightning would almost certainly strike. She'd finally get to experience that rush that made life worth living. Ransom was certain of it.

Like you were certain she'd enjoy skydiving?

He forced himself to consider it. Annaliese was good-natured, nice—and vulnerable. Would he be helping her by rushing her into bed with the guy, no matter how exciting he knew she'd find it, how much fun she'd have?

Or would he be unintentionally hurting her instead? *Again.*

He shook his head. *This is different.* This time he could see how she trembled on the brink of excitement. She was ready.

Maybe *he* was the one who wasn't ready. *Trying to talk myself out of helping her bed the pirate because I'm scared shitless they'll click? That I'll be the one left on the outside looking in?*

This isn't a wedding, idiot. It's just sex. Help her.

Fuck it. The dancer might not be her one and only, but he could give her a fun time. If their coupling turned them into a couple, Ransom would be happy for her.

He turned his gaze to the pirate. *And if the guy turns out to be no more than a rugged face and great body—if her* hurts *her—I'll beat the snot out of him.*

And he'd be there to catch her.

Ransom felt Annaliese's gaze on him again. Flicking eyes back to her, he remembered the first time he *wasn't* there to catch her and winced.

He'd discovered the thrill of jumping from a tire swing into the pond on his family estate, and wanted to share it with her, his best friend.

She'd been giddy and flushed, exactly like this. Excited.

But she'd released too late, flown too far, plummeted too deep. She nearly hadn't made it to the surface.

The moment he'd realized she was in trouble, he'd dived down for her. Grabbed her arm, pulling her safely to air.

Physically, she'd been fine, but in some ways he'd reached her too late. The scare wiped out any initial excitement for her. She'd never gone swimming with him again. The tire swing was abandoned.

But she was an adult now. He studied her face, lit with the same combination of terror and electrified joy as that day, flying from the tire swing. Almost screaming *help me take the chance.*

Back then, the terror had won. But here was another chance—for them both. Her chance for the thrill to win out over the fear. His chance to help her, if he was man enough.

Ransom *had* to help her seize this opportunity to *live.*

This time, I'll be there to catch you, Annie. Promise.

*   *   *

Annaliese turned to Ransom. The dancer raised feelings and urges in her, so hot and fast it overwhelmed her. She knew her confusion showed in her eyes because the moment their gazes met, Ransom nodded.

As usual, he seemed to know what to do. He grabbed her arm and pulled her into motion.

Well, "pull" implied resistance. When Ransom wanted to go somewhere, he didn't have to drag her, she came willingly. *Unless it involves leaping through the air or moving past the speed of sound, that is.*

He led her around scurrying caterers and through the crowd still avidly watching the dancer to the doorway where he'd been greeting guests. Straight through the entry foyer and into the dining room, he hooked a left, leading her parallel to the long formal table to reach his kitchen.

Kitchen. She snorted as he led her through a pair of swinging doors. Like the word "pulled", kitchen wasn't quite right when Ransom was involved. "Kitchen" implied a snug homey room, but Ransom's was huge, filled with monster chrome refrigerators and professional ovens bigger than most houses.

Tugging her into the middle of the room, he faced her and took her by the bare arms, his long fingers sending tremors of pleasure along her skin. "You like that guy?"

"Guy?" Her shoulders knotted. Sure, she was glad Ransom had understood her confusion about the dancer and had gotten her out of there. But that didn't mean she wanted her friend to go further, to try to *solve* her problem.

Ransom's solutions tended to involve pushing her out of a plane.

She pretended ignorance. "What guy?"

"You know which guy. The stripper."

"Exotic dancer," she said automatically.

"Did he strip off clothes or not?" Ransom released her to wave his palms. "Never mind. Doesn't matter what we call him, you want him. I know you do."

"*Want* him?" Annaliese hoped he didn't mean what she thought he meant. Though really, this was *Ransom.* He could only mean sex...and at the thought, her mind replayed her last image of the pirate, muscles sheening as he did push-ups, her wondering if that was how he'd look pumping over her in bed... She cleared her throat. "Well, maybe. I do need some things done around my apartment and he looks capable..." She dribbled off at Ransom's raised eyebrow.

Yeah, he means sex.

She gave an irked shrug, trying to cover the fact that her pelvis felt like liquid fire. "So, I admire a human body. A male...muscular..." She cleared her throat. "A human body. So what?"

"So, I'll help you do it."

"Help me do what?"

"What do you think? Fuck him."

The floor dropped from under her. All her churning acid desire pooled into an already-on-fire pussy, boiling out of control. She vented it in a hiss of frustration. "F-f-fuh-what...? Ransom, I don't even know the man. And in case you hadn't noticed, all of the women and half the men in there were drooling over him. Even if I wanted a one-night stand, what makes you think, of all the people he could ask for s-sex, he'd ask me?"

"Simple. You don't wait for him to ask. You seduce him."

"I *what?*"

"It won't be hard. I saw how he looked at you." Ransom's expression turned smug. "He wants you too."

Heat roared through her, tailing in a long, lush shiver. She couldn't meet her friend's eyes. "N-no. You don't know that. You *can't.*"

"Really?" He chucked a finger under her chin and raised her gaze to his. "Annaliese. Who am I? And what do I know about?"

She was already shaking her head. "Even if you're right, I can't. Granny always said, 'Don't date a man you wouldn't marry.'"

Ransom made an exasperated noise and dropped his hand. "Annaliese, you're not going to marry the man, you're just going to fuck him."

Need twisted in her pelvis. *Fuck him.* Deep, seething urges wrung her insides until desire was nearly pain.

But she was also shocked at Ransom's bare language, and anguished that he, of all people, would push her into a tryst with another man—and not even a date, but sex with a stranger that degraded romance and love into animal lust.

Her feelings collided inside her and resolved into a glare, aimed at Ransom.

He waved an apologetic hand. "Yes, sorry. But you're interested in him, I know you are. And he's interested in you. Why not at least follow up on that? Go meet him."

"Meet him?"

"Yeah. Who knows? Maybe you'll find out he's the kind of guy you'd want to marry." Surprisingly, a grimace flashed across Ransom's handsome features, gone in an instant. "Just go meet him, Annie. Doesn't have to be for sex or even anything long-term. Say hi. Offer him a drink. I'd guess he'd be thirsty after all that physical activity." A wry grin twisted his lips.

"*You* offer him a drink." Her gaze twitched away. "I've got this party to supervise—"

"You're scared—I get that."

"What?" Her eyes switched back, landing on him with shock. Most of the time it seemed Ransom was too busy with his exciting life for dull little Annie, but sometimes, like now, he proved he cared, seeing things inside her that were buried so deep even she didn't know they were there until he pointed them out.

His expression was a mix of frustration, sadness, impatience, and a compassion so warm she wanted to cry.

He gently tapped her nose. "Don't worry, I'll help."

"Help? Like you 'helped' me with the school pool high dive?" She mimed a shove and run.

He gave her a quick apologetic grin. "You had to do it to pass gym class. And you survived."

"After I coughed out half the pool."

"I won't push you at him and run. I'll stay. I'll be there for you."

Hope came with an oxygenating breath. If Ransom wouldn't abandon her, she might just be able to survive meeting the handsome pirate. "You promise? You promise you'll be there...?" She dribbled off as what she was actually saying hit her. "You'll be *there*? As in, right there?" She couldn't seem to wrap her head around the enormity of what he was suggesting. Good to know he wouldn't shove her and run. But the alternative... "You'll be *right there while I try to seduce a strange, nearly naked man?"*

Ransom shrugged and had the grace to blush a little. "I might learn something."

She yelped, "You're joking!"

"Please, Annaliese, just give it a try? Go meet him. And if more happens…" He clasped her shoulders again. "I'll help."

There it was again. He'd *help?* Help with meeting the stranger?

Or help with touching, kissing, *fucking him…?*

Dear lord. If she wasn't mistaken, Ransom had finally—*finally*—offered to go to bed with her. Her stomach exploded with need. She clenched, thigh muscles, belly muscles, and licked suddenly dry lips. The idea shimmered on the edge of perfection…

Except to go to bed with the man of her dreams, she had to first seduce a stranger.

Fear drained her of heat. "No. I-I can't." The words exploded from her. "I'm sorry, Ransom, but even with you helping, I simply can't."

With a sigh, he stepped back, his hands dropping from her. His disappointed expression stung her. He said, "Okay, I understand. I'll leave you to your party managing."

He turned and shoved out the swinging doors.

Leaving her cold inside and wishing with all her might that she could be the exciting seductress Ransom wanted her to be.

Chapter Four

Annaliese turned her back to the kitchen doors, still swinging from Ransom's stormy exit, and stumbled to the center of the room, hugging her bare arms. She wanted to throw up.

Just try, Ransom had said.

He wanted her to go to bed with a stranger.

I can't. Granny...

But Granny wasn't here. Ransom was. And he was so let down that she wouldn't even try.

She'd do anything, *anything* to erase that disappointed expression.

Even seduce a stranger?

Her shivering increased. She jammed her clammy hands under her arms and tried not to cry. How could she not even try? Especially since she'd finally done it, finally gotten Ransom's adrenaline pumping. He'd been so excited by the idea of her and the pirate. She knew it from the sparkle in his eyes, the fire in his gaze.

Snuffed when she said no.

She swallowed a big block of ice. That had nearly killed her.

Swallowing again, she forced herself to stand straighter, to drop her hands and relax. Consciously she took deep breaths, aping confidence, hoping to fool her body into feeling the real thing.

Couldn't she at least try? She knew the basics of attraction and sex. She could try to seduce one man—especially one who was already supposedly interested, right? Even though she didn't know him, didn't love him, she could go to bed with one sexy hunk of muscular dancer?

Wrap my legs around his powerful waist as I take him inside me, again and again...? Her sex clenched at the thought. She shifted her stance, panties rubbing, making her very aware of how wet she was.

Damn it. She loved *Ransom.*

So why was she drenched at the thought of bedding that pirate?

*   *   *

Building to his big finish, Jack whipped the steel prop sword from its sheath, stabbed it at the ceiling, and struck a fierce pose, capped by the last cymbal crash of music.

In the crowd, he saw the woman's back as she left with the blond man. Applause broke out, but Jack's heart plummeted.

A SEAL does not give up on the mission. He gritted his teeth. *Follow them.*

Sheathing his sword, he gave Lilly a signal that he was heading out.

She acknowledged him with a nod, a considering gleam in her eye. She'd seen him lock gazes with the woman, then.

Good and bad news. Lilly would help him by covering for him—for now. But when he returned to the office, she'd pump him for details. Lilly had techniques that even the CIA shuddered at.

Deal with it later. Focus on the mission now. He headed for the door where he'd seen the angel disappear. Lilly followed with the cart.

The crowd surged around him, female hands and arms reaching for him, trying to stop him.

"Comin' through!" Lilly trundled past with her bulky cart, knocking arms away.

He sped up to trot parallel to her, taking advantage of the space she bought him until he was within reach of the doorway.

Bottleneck. His brain lit up *adverse terrain* just as the narrow passage scraped him away from the protection of Lilly's cart.

Leaving him prey to the nightmare of arms.

Hands fastened onto his biceps, his wrists. One grabbed for his sheathed sword—not the metal one.

Calling on all his training, he twisted his hips and wrists at the same moment that he flexed his biceps. The woman grabbing for his sword missed. The two hanging onto his arms could no longer contain the width of his biceps. His wrists slipped from the last two, popping through the place where thumb and forefinger met, the weakest part of a grip.

Free, he dashed out into the corridor with a half-second of lead time, and suddenly realized he had no idea which way to go.

Assess. He was in a foyer. Stairs to his left. Outside door to his right. Straight ahead was another doorway.

The front door opened. A cool breeze raised his nipples as more elegantly dressed men and women entered.

They stared at him and he wondered why, until he remembered he was wearing nothing but his pouch, a patch, and pirate boots.

But that answered that, didn't it? *Find cover, sailor.* He dashed across the foyer, nipping through the doorway.

He found himself in a large dining room, a glossy embassy-size table dominating the space.

One exit, a pair of swinging doors in back.

He was considering his next move when the doors swung wide and the aristocratic blond strode through.

Blue eyes widened on Jack, and the blond's steps stuttered, but then his gaze flicked away and, regaining his stride, he brushed by Jack apparently without seeing him.

Arrogant ass. Jack stood there, clenching fists until it struck him—last he'd seen the angelic woman, she'd been with the blond. Did that mean...?

She might be through those doors.

His belly contracted with barely contained need.

Using every ounce of his rigorous military training and willpower, he reined his lust in. *I'm just meeting her. A woman like her, I have to take it slow and easy. Gentle.*

Gentle, right. When all he wanted to do was drape her over this table and bury himself between her thighs until they were both shouting in ecstasy.

Don't fuck up the mission, sailor. He strode to the swinging doors, paused, then pressed back both doors and went in.

The woman stood alone in the middle of a sleek kitchen, her slender back to him. He wondered for a moment where the food was coming from, remembered the caterers, then wondered why they weren't using this room as a staging area.

Oh, well, his gain.

As if she sensed his presence, she turned.

Their eyes met. A pang of desire speared his gut. She had the sweetest, most beguiling sugar-brown eyes...her pretty lips moved.

"H-hello."

Her voice was sweet too, drugging him like honey with the desire to taste her, to lick and nip and kiss her, to *roll* himself in her sweetness...

And she was staring at him, waiting for him to speak. Right. SEALS knew how to attain their objectives, and sometimes that even included language.

He managed a croaked, "Hi."

She shivered visibly, as if he'd caressed his palms along her bare arms.

His cock jerked. It *liked* that idea. "I'm Jack."

"My name's Annaliese." She cleared her throat. "Um, you dance well."

At that, her gaze skimmed his body, almost as if she couldn't help herself.

"Thanks." He preened under her gaze. "I saw you in the main room and wanted to meet you." He held out his hand and crossed the distance between them on winged feet.

Shyly, she took his hand in a brief clasp. Hers was small and soft in his and slightly damp.

He couldn't help imagining those warm, slick fingers grasping his erection. At the thought, he goosed her hand with a little squeeze.

A gasp escaped her. She started to slide her hand from his in retreat.

Damn it. Suddenly desperate to not lose even this small connection, he laid his hand on her shoulder to delay her. If she really wanted to pull away he'd let her, but touching her, smelling her...heavens, her scent was like cinnamon sugar, as sweet as she looked. He took a deep, appreciative breath, his lips curving in pleasure.

She froze, her eyes flying up to his face. But at least she stopped pulling away.

Close up, she really was a small thing, compared to him at any rate. It would make sweeping her off her feet easy. Carrying her upstairs, laying her gently down on a bed to cover her with kisses...

She was waiting for him to speak, to maybe explain why he'd put his hand on her shoulder.

He racked his mind for something brilliant to say. His brain was all jumpy and dazzled and all he could think of was idiotic things like how good she smelled and how badly he wanted to fuck her. He settled on the banal, "So, do you live here?"

"This house?" Shaking her head, she smiled. "No. I'm not that rich. My friend Ransom owns the place. But I threw the birthday party for him."

"Ransom?" So. The enemy...pardon, *the blond man* had a name. He was the birthday boy, and she'd thrown the party for him. Bad news. That meant she and the blond were close enough to throw parties for each other.

But she'd also said *friend*. Not husband or fiancé or even boyfriend. Simply friend, no commitment implied.

Jack's whole body lifted. He had a chance with her. The joy heating his blood carried him a breath from touching her.

She started to edge away, as if he'd frightened her.

His heart stopped.

Then she steeled her spine and stayed where she was. His heart burst with happiness—then slowed as reason overtook him.

She was acting like a skittish colt, not a woman who wanted him as much as he wanted her. Or like a raw recruit afraid of firearms. Forcing herself to go through with firing the deadly weapon though she didn't want to.

Forcing herself to stay near him, maybe even only enduring his touch.

His bubble of joy deflated.

Then she put her tiny hand on his shoulder, lightly, like the soft kiss of a butterfly.

Suddenly, his whole body shuddering in a fire of need, he didn't give a shit about anything except that she was giving him a chance. An opening to get to know her better; a chance to charm her.

New mission—charm the hell out of her.

She said, barely more than a whisper, "I have a confession."

"You do?" His voice was a rasp of desire. *Charm, damn you.*

Like a small bird, her other hand flit to his waist. "I wanted to meet you too." She lifted herself on her toes, offering her lips.

A torpedo exploded in his groin. All thoughts of charming her went out the window. With a groan, he bent, and it was only the last gasp of his conscious will that stopped him from claiming her with a raw shout of triumph.

Gentle, damn it. Tender. He brushed his mouth against hers—and groaned. Her lips were sweeter than all the rest of her put together.

Intense pleasure rode him in a shudder. She was soft and nice and everything he'd ever dreamed of in the hot swelter of duty stations.

Updated mission—make her *his*.

His arms went around her, and he drew her in.

Her weight shifted suddenly, her hips popping back as if she was shocked by contact with him—or rather, with his raging bulge. That was good because, if she knew what his erection meant, she wasn't completely innocent. But it was bad because it also meant he was a step or two ahead of her, arousal-wise.

Yanking hard on his control, he tried to get her used to the feel of him with repeated soft kisses, pressing his lips gently against hers, brushes that lengthened like the beat of a bird's wings on liftoff.

Easing her into his taste, his feel, until, stepping in, she leaned her pelvis against his and gave a tentative wiggle.

His cock shouted with delight.

Then she walked her fingers up his chest like something out of a corny movie—her *cold* fingers.

Sanity swam up through his fogged brain—she was trying to *seduce* him. Trying to seduce him when, from the cold fingers, she was still afraid.

If it had been anyone but her, he'd have shrugged and let her try. Maybe even helped her along.

But from her closed mouth pecks, her clumsy, almost puppy-like wiggling, and especially her cold fingers, she wasn't seducing him because she wanted to.

He had no idea why she was doing it, but regretfully, he'd have to walk away.

Even the thought hurt like a combat knife to the gut.

At least now he knew her name. *Annaliese.* He'd have to try again under more favorable conditions, like when he wasn't sporting a hard-on the size of Rhode Island in a pouch that barely covered him.

"Well." He cleared his throat and straightened from her.

Her hands fell away from him. He had to consciously release her. As he did, his fingers tingled. They'd never forget the feel of her creamy skin, her curvy body.

He cleared his throat again. "It was nice meeting you. See you again sometime."

He turned and took a couple reluctant steps away.

An instant of stunned silence was followed by the scurry of feet. "Wait!"

He paused without turning. "What?"

"You said you wanted to meet me. D-don't you want to get to know me better? To...m-make love?"

The little hesitations in her words tugged at him. Damn it, it was hard to be noble when she was so deliciously sweet, and she offered herself to him practically on a platter. He forced himself to say, "Sure. To all of the above. But some other time, when you really want to."

And then, though it was the hardest thing in the world, he willed his thigh muscles to lift his leg, to take another step. He had to get out of here, before his cock grabbed him and spun him, demanding he snap up what she was offering.

"Wait," she said again, her soft, small hand landing on his naked back.

Her fingers might have been live wires connected to a car battery. Every muscle in his whole body seized with need, gluing him to the spot.

"If you don't want me," she whispered, her breath warm against his back, "what do you want?"

He shook his head and gave a laugh, no humor in it. "Don't get me wrong. I want you. But my first impression of you... I thought you were nice. I still do. This isn't you."

"It's me," she said quickly. "Ransom only..." No more words came.

But suddenly, with a fire that was nearly rage, Jack knew. He knew why she was trying to seduce him. He clenched fists. "The birthday boy put you up to it? What reason could he possibly have to do such a thing?" He still couldn't turn, couldn't look at her.

"I-I'm not sure. I know he enjoys danger. Craves it. I think...I think he wants me to be a thrill-seeker, too."

Jack's spine snapped so straight it hurt. She saw him as a dangerous thrill, not a man? "Have fun with some other chump."

Fury and pain drove him toward the door. He'd taken two strides when her hurt little voice stopped him.

"Jack, *please*."

The pitter-patter of feet scurrying after him alerted him. He knew before she touched him that she'd reached out.

She caught his forearm, her fingers barely curving around the thews. That soft, small hand... He choked down a groan of pure lust.

"Don't go." She whispered it.

"You told me what Ransom wants." He finally couldn't stand it anymore and twisted to face her. "What do *you* want?"

His anger died, seeing the pleading in her glossy eyes, her lips rosy with emotion.

More gently, he repeated, "What do *you* want, Annaliese? What do you from me?"

Gingerbread gaze dropping, she murmured, "I don't expect you to understand, but Ransom said if you and I...he'd help, if you and I..." She stopped, blushing bright red.

Sex. She means sex.

Immediately he got hard again. She was talking about sex *with him*.

Idiot. The blond's name is in the mix.

Meaning the blond was in the mix?

He recalled her words. *If you and I... Ransom said he'd help.*

Jack, already attuned to her in some basic way, suddenly understood. If he took Annaliese to bed, in some way he'd also be taking her desire for Ransom to bed too.

Having sex with the blond through *me?*

Not. Happening. He opened his mouth to snarl a *no fucking way.*

Then she raised her eyes. The pleading there was so raw. He knew that look. He'd seen it in his own eyes when he was in-country, every morning when he'd shaved, before he put his game face on.

She's dreamed of loving this Ransom as long as I've dreamed of a woman like her.

But taking the ghost of another man to bed with them? What kind of start to a relationship was that?

It's at least a start, asshat. Answer this, sailor. Do you want her? More to the point, do you want her happy?

One answer to that—yes.

So, okay. Give it a try. At the very least it would make Annaliese happy. He'd have to figure out some way to deal with the blond.

Then a thought flamed through him. "Your friend will help? Help *how,* exactly?"

Taking Annaliese to bed with the ghost of the blond was one thing—but bedding the man too? Entirely another matter.

He rigidly pushed away the fact that his erection had not died at the thought.

*   *   *

When Ransom left Annaliese in the kitchen, shoving an exasperated hand through his hair, he went to find the big dancer. Her internal grandma wouldn't let her have a good time—and that was two

51

and a half strikes against Granny for Annaliese still carting around that date-marry bullshit, shutting down her sexuality.

But maybe firing up Annie's libido with another eyeful of those shredded muscles would do the job for her.

And damn. Here the pirate was, looking as though he'd steam through the dining room like a battleship.

Well good. One less thing he'd have to handle.

Brushing past the man, Ransom headed for the main room to rejoin the party—and remembered his promise to Annaliese. *I'll help. I won't run away.*

Fuck. He wasn't sure what fun she'd have with him there, but he'd promised. He spun on his heel to return to the kitchen, realizing in the nick of time that, Annaliese aside, the *pirate* wasn't the kind to take interference from another man.

Ransom paused. How could he help Annaliese but not interfere?

He snapped fingers as an idea hit him. His home was equipped with a security system, including several interior cameras. He could watch from his laptop to make sure everything went well. Swoop in to save her if she needed him, like he'd promised, but in the meantime let nature—and the pirate—do their thing.

Sitting in his home's upstairs saferoom, Ransom watched the kitchen feed with a grimace. The two were dancing around each other like overpadded toddlers in their first karate sparring match. A brief kiss raised Ransom's heart rate...until the man broke it off. Ransom turned up the volume.

The pirate's growl greeted him, pure sex, sending unexpected frissons along his skin.

"It was nice meeting you. See you again sometime."

And the damned man turned to leave.

Ransom shot to his feet, but when Annaliese had the good sense to chase the dancer, he snapped off the volume, sank back into his chair and watched body language.

Screw it, what man and woman, attracted that much, took so long to get down to it? Ransom had a good mind to march down there and smack their fool heads—well, maybe not their heads. Their bottoms, good hard spanks that would carry up to their brains...

The image caught him, his hand on soft female and roped male buttocks, and gave him a spurt of arousal.

Then the pirate spun and again headed for the door, and Ransom knew he had to act. He dashed out of the room, pounding down the stairs toward the kitchen.

*   *   *

Even growling in anger, the pirate Jack had the most gorgeous baritone voice in the world. Annaliese could listen to him talk forever.

But she might never hear him again if he walked out on her now.

Fingers clamped on his forearm, she searched his face, her own on fire, her pulse a rapid rat-a-tat in her ears.

Fury was in that dark one-eyed gaze—along with pain.

She couldn't believe how badly she'd blown it.

Well, why should she be surprised? She knew about befriending a guy, and even how to accept offers of sex, thanks to a couple well-meaning friends with horny brothers.

But making love, much less seducing a strong, attractive man like Jack?

Gazing at him hurt. She averted her eyes. Her awkwardness and embarrassment were painful enough, but knowing he understood why she'd done this and the fact that she'd accidentally hurt him? That was agony.

Somehow, in the short time since their gazes fused in the living room, she'd come to care about his feelings—not just the caring she had for any soul, but something more personal.

I could come to love Jack, if I didn't already love Ransom. The realization surprised her.

Speaking of Ransom... He'd know what to do now, but he wasn't here. Shoving her off the diving board and running out on her again—

"What the fuck's taking you so long?"

Her friend's strong tenor preceded him slapping open the swinging doors like a cowboy coming into a barroom fight.

Immediately her heart rate steadied, her core warming, bringing sensation back, turning her fear into the possibility of pleasure.

As Ransom entered, Jack spun in front of her, as if *he'd* protect *her* from her friend.

She nearly laughed, but the way Jack flared, his muscles pumping, robbed her of breath.

"Well, come on," Ransom said. "You both want to. What's the holdup?"

Annaliese's face heated again. Did he have to be so obvious? She peeked out from behind Jack's bulk. Ransom had stopped a few steps in, fists on hips, glaring at them both. Impossible man.

She reminded herself he was doing what he thought best for her. "Ransom, this is Jack. Jack, this is my *friend,* Ransom." She emphasized the word. Jack didn't seem to like Ransom, and she could sense the danger in the pirate. Jack was big and honed like a knife. Ransom was elegant and slender. If Jack erupted in violence, she knew who was winning, and who was bruising.

On second thought, maybe it would be better if she were between the two. She inched around, sneaking herself in front of Jack. "Ransom, we were only talking."

"I *know.*" Ransom rolled his eyes. "That's the problem." He ate up the distance between them in a couple long strides to put a brotherly hand on her shoulder. Muttered, "You've hooked the fish, now reel him in." His gaze flashed from her to the man behind her.

Jack audibly snarled.

Yikes. She twisted to flutter an *it's-okay* smile at the pirate. Then she turned back to Mr. Obvious. "I don't know what you mean." She had to force the words through gritted teeth.

"I mean there are all those empty bedrooms upstairs, made up and ready to go—including your usual room. So let's go." He slung a friendly arm around her waist and urged her into motion, strolling toward the doors.

"*Let's?*" Confused hope freed her legs. "You and me?"

"You and the pirate."

Acid hit her stomach, and she put on the brakes. "No, wait."

"Why?" Ransom arched one blond brow at her. "You're attracted to him, he's attracted to you. Go have fun together."

"I-I can't..." Any courage or resolution to seduce Jack dissolved in the fear-soaked idea of screwing up with the big man again. She glanced behind her.

Jack's frown held a crinkle of pain, the pupil of his uncovered eye constricted, as if her rejection hurt him even more than her botched seduction.

Her insides roiled unpleasantly. She didn't want to hurt the pirate and really didn't like disappointing Ransom. Yet when it came down to it, she wasn't *ready* for this. She felt like a scared little bunny, her fear so acrid she could *smell* it...

She stunk, a turn-off—and an excuse.

"I mean, I can't *yet*." Breathlessly, she rattled off, "I'm not saying no, but I've been working all day on this party, and I reek, so I need to wash first." The more she thought about it, the more she liked the idea. If she dashed upstairs for a quick shower, she could not only avoid the immediate confrontation, she might be able to delay until one or both men forgot about her. "So, I'll just run upstairs, okay?"

Suiting action to words, she skedaddled.

Leaving the two men alone with each other.

Chapter Five

Warm water sluiced down Annaliese's bare skin. She couldn't believe her near escape—and that a part of her was disappointed she had.

Standing in the tub shower of the bath en-suite of "her" room—one of Ransom's many guest bedrooms, but the one he held open for her exclusive use—that strange, foreign part of her wished she were still down there with the big pirate. That she'd gone through with the terrifying…thrilling…prospect of having sex with Jack.

But the larger part of her was relieved.

Really?

Really, she told herself firmly. Avoidance was the best answer. That way, nobody got hurt, not Ransom, not Jack, and especially not her.

She shampooed and rinsed, then put conditioner in her hair. Leaving that to work, she pumped face soap into her palm then paused. That even a part of her wished she'd gone through with it—did that mean Ransom was right? Did he know her better than she knew herself?

Did she really want to jump into bed with a virtual stranger, just for the excitement?

A shimmy in her sex seemed to say *oh, yes.*

So what if she'd gone through with it?

Jack seemed pretty nice—for a powerful, dangerous sort of guy. Sure, she was scared, but it wasn't like he was going to hurt her in the middle of Ransom's party, with Ransom knowing she was with him. If she had to have nearly anonymous sex with someone, she could do a lot worse.

And from his dancing, Jack certainly knew how to use his hips. Another, harder thrill hit her low. The slow roll of abs, his jutting, barely covered erection below, astonishing everyone by growing even bigger... Her thighs were getting slick, and it wasn't the shower.

What part of escape *don't I understand?*

Briskly she scrubbed face soap between her palms, working up a lather before distracting herself washing her face.

* * *

I need a wash first.

The image of Annaliese running a soapy cloth over her bare skin made Jack, still standing in the kitchen, want to follow her like a puppy, to replace the washcloth with his tongue.

He'd have clenched his eyes shut in pain, but the moment she disappeared, the blond man turned on him.

"What the fuck's wrong with you?" Ransom snarled. "She's pretty, she's smart, and she wants you. Go give her a good time."

"Pretty, smart—and she's also nice," Jack snarled back. "You, however, are an asshole. I'm not bedding her because she loves *you,* jackass."

To his surprise, pain flashed across the blond's aristocratic features. "Yeah, I know. And if I could turn myself the man she needs, I'd do it in a heartbeat. But I'm not built that way."

Jack caught the other man's pain, but his compassion was drowned out by a hope surging in his chest. "Oh? What kind of man does she need?"

"Stable. Strong. Secure." The blond nailed him with his gaze. "You."

Jack's hope intensified. But it didn't matter, did it? Her heart was set on Ransom. Jack's chest deflated.

Her attachment to the blond man wasn't simply a passing fancy. He'd seen in her eyes how deeply her feelings ran. If he'd doubted his read of her, she'd shown him just how far out of her comfort zone she'd go for the blond, hadn't she?

Trying to seduce a man she didn't want—from her cold hands, a man she even feared.

His insides crumbled. The woman he wanted to love—she hated and feared him.

"You're wrong," the blond said. "It's her own insecurities she's afraid of, not you."

Jack's jaw dropped. "Excused me. Did you just read my mind?"

"No, but where Annaliese is concerned...let's just say I'm a bit more observant and a lot more protective. So if you hurt her, I'm going to kick your ass."

Jack found himself raising palms. "I don't want to hurt her. I only wanted to meet her. Maybe ask her for a date."

Blond brows arched, the other man's gaze raked scornfully over Jack's naked torso. "Dressed like that?"

Embarrassment made Jack snap, "I didn't have much choice. I didn't think to bring a change of clothes in my dickpouch."

The other man's gaze dropped and riveted to the aforementioned dickpouch, a grin touching his lips. "That size? You might have been able to fit two changes." His eyes rose and his grin disappeared. "Look—Jack, is it? Jack, I watched you dance. I know you can show Annaliese a good time. And I know she wants it. Needs it. But *you* are the one who is going to have to get her started."

"Why are you so determined about this?"

The blond half-raised his hands, forming the V of an almost-shrug. "She works all the damned time. I want her to relax a little. Have some fun."

Jack frowned. "Her idea of fun might be different than yours, you know."

"Not a chance. I know Annaliese—I've known her all my life."

"That doesn't make you an expert."

Something in the blond's aristocratic pose seemed to break. He shot straight and got in Jack's face, going so far as to shake an angry fist under his nose. "Look here, you fucking know-it-all—"

"Don't try it." Jack had only to stare down with narrowed eyes and put on his hardest expression.

"Fine." Jaw clenching, the other man visibly reined himself in. "But listen up. I'm only saying this once..

"I'm all ears."

"Annie's *idea* of fun is what she thinks is *appropriate*—not what she'll actually enjoy if she dares to get excited. She needs help getting rid of her Granny-imposed boundaries. I'm asking you to show her a good time because I care about her, even love her, in my own way. Now are you going to go up there and bed her, or not?"

"You have a strange way of showing your love, pushing her into another man's embrace."

The blond glared. "You gonna help her or not?"

"Not." Jack leaned back, arms crossed. "*You* might think it's okay, but I'm not pushing her where she doesn't want to go. Whether it's good for her or not."

The blond made a noise of frustration. "You're as stubborn as she is, aren't you? Tell you what. I'm going upstairs to get her motor revved—and then I'm heading back to the party. You can drive her to paradise or leave her idling, your choice."

He slapped the swinging doors open and strode from the kitchen.

Chapter Six

"Fuck." Jack clenched fists. The blond was going to rev Annaliese's motor? If that meant what Jack thought...touching her creamy flesh, seeing her sweet face contorted in pleasure...

"Double fuck. Wait up! I'm coming."

Ransom slapped the kitchen doors open and leaned in with a grin. "Well, I should certainly hope so. And for your sake, I hope Annie is coming too."

*   *   *

Annaliese scrubbed her forehead and cheeks and eyes extra-hard, as if by stimulating her head she could distract herself from the heavy pooling of desire in her pelvis.

Fingers massaged into her jaw. "You missed a couple spots," Ransom said.

She shrieked. Her eyes sprang open, muscles tensing...except her jaw. She hadn't known she was grinding her teeth until he'd relieved the pressure.

She'd have been self-conscious about being nude with a guy, even Ransom, her best friend, but his gaze was single-mindedly on his work, all above the collar bone. Her shoulders eased and her lids drooped. "How'd you get in?" It came out more like "Ow oo eh ih" under his rolling thumbs.

"You left your door unlocked. I could see you were stuck in your head, and I didn't want to disturb you. But punkin', you have some tight muscles here. I couldn't leave you hurting." Ransom leaned in through the open shower door—he must've silently opened it—to knead her jaw more deeply. His coat was off and his sleeves rolled to mid-forearm, but the water was still dampening him.

"Stop. You're getting wet."

"All in a good cause. You should wash the rest of you. That reek, you know. I'm sure Jack won't mind, but you might."

Jack. At the thought of the pirate, her belly again flooded with a wash of need and fear. Damn it, she was a mass of conflicted emotions, wanting, *needing* so badly it almost burned, but fear freezing her from taking that first step, even for Ransom. She opened her mouth to say no. "Um, yeah, about that..."

He reached past her to grab a scented bar from the groove in the tub surround. The scent of his shampoo and aftershave wafted into her nostrils as he went past, his heat warming her naked, wet flesh.

All thoughts disappeared. *I was about to tell him something important...*

He straightened, and the light lime-and-male scent of him, again wafting past, dashed every last word from her vocabulary. He handed the bar to her. "Take the soap, Annaliese."

Numb fingers grabbed the bar, digits she barely realized were hers, and automatically started soaping her belly, tiny repetitive circles that didn't wash anything except one square inch of skin.

Ransom *tsked*. "You're really that scared? He's not a real pirate, you know." Grinning to take the sting out of it, he slid the soap from her still-numb fingers, and began to soap his own hands.

"Wh-what are you doing?

"I'm your wingman, Annie," he murmured. "You need help revving up. I'll get your motor started. Then you can take off and *fly*. Turn around."

Hesitantly, she offered him her back.

He put his palms on her the small of her back, fingers kneading the muscles, working up.

"Oh, that feels good." As knots of tension fell out, she collapsed limply against the surround and enjoyed. She'd always hoped *someday* Ransom would touch her as a lover. This wasn't someday, but it was as close as she'd get, and she was happy.

Until she heard a distinct, dangerous baritone growl.

Stomach flying into her throat, she jerked around.

Ransom blocked her view. With a grin, he helpfully bent to run his soapy hands down her flanks—revealing the pirate watching, his searing, one-eyed gaze licking like a flame over her nude body.

"Oh...oh heavens." Stars exploded in her belly, terror and shock and thrill all jumbled together. Automatically, she covered herself with her arms. Her nipples poked her skin.

"Don't worry about him, punkin'." Straightening, Ransom thrust fingers into her wet hair. "I'm revving your engine. He'll help you get airborne." He leaned in and pressed his mouth to hers.

Shock melted into surprise. *Ransom is kissing me. At last.*

His mouth was warm, soft, and as beguiling as lemon meringue. Her eyes slid shut and her arms fell as sensation claimed her.

She'd dreamed of this moment since she'd known boys were different. Her exploding stars eased into fireworks of joy.

When he had her panting and dizzy, his mouth lifted. "Your turn."

She didn't know what he meant until another mouth closed on hers, hard and demanding. Stunning instead of drugging. Whiskey in place of lemon meringue.

Jack.

A hot tongue thrust between her lips, powerful, irrefutable. Ransom's kiss must've drugged her because instead of shrieking and trying to run away, she opened her mouth to the onslaught. The pirate boarded her with a kiss to conquer. His tongue drove deep, infusing her with his taste. She groaned as her muscles yielded.

Plumbing clunked, Ransom turning off the shower because the water stopped. Annaliese roused to object—until Jack swept her off her feet, lifting over the lip of the tub. Settling her into his arms, he carried her out of the bathroom.

The shock of naked skin to naked skin jolted through her, raising every hair on her body, stiffening her nipples to sharp points, making her pussy weep naked desire.

Shocked at her own searing reaction, she wriggled to be set down—which only stimulated her worse. Her heart hammered into overdrive as he carried her into the bedroom. Before she knew it, he was lowering her onto the bed—slowly, almost frame by frame. Maybe giving her time to object, but all she could do was pant at his triceps and biceps working under his bronzed skin as he lowered her easily, as if she weighed nothing. *Damn, the man is strong.*

He set her down. The bedspread was silky and cool under her damp, naked buttocks. She opened her mouth to protest getting the bedclothes wet when she caught sight of Ransom behind the dancer.

His blue gaze…it held nothing of what she'd have imagined. No mischievous grin, no lusty leer. Not even a mild flush of adrenaline.

No, her friend's heart was in his eyes, like a man pleading for a second chance.

Before she could ask *a second chance for what?* the mattress dented like a planet hit it, and Jack climbed onto the bed with her. She fell back onto her elbows.

Straddling her, he came onto his knees above her, leering one-eyed down at her, like a true conquering pirate.

Her heart hammered, her breasts rose and fell rapidly as she lay beneath him. He bent, again slowly, so that she could have stopped him—until his hand threaded her hair, holding her for his kiss.

This wasn't Ransom tangling his slender fingers in her tresses. Wasn't his light, beguiling kiss.

No, Jack's big hand cupped her whole head. It made her aware on a primitive level how big he was compared to her. And when his mouth crashed onto hers, he kissed her as if he was trying to imprint her very soul.

Her breathing, already ragged, sped into a series of panted gulps. She'd never been so unnerved, so roiling, so...what?...in her life. Excited?

Excited seemed too tame a word for the fury, the passion, storming her blood. Ransom might enjoy his love this extreme, this fevered, but Annaliese was used to a blander diet. She put her hands up, to stop Jack, or at least slow him down.

Her palms landed on his big chest. Muscles like boulders, covered only in a thin layer of velvety skin, met her palms. The pirate was pure power, sheathed in warm cream. She'd never felt a man like him before. A thrill skewered her belly. Her arms trembled, and her desire flamed, her need rising in a groan.

He growled his encouragement. Still kneeling over her, he caressed fingers down her cheek, the sheer gentleness electrifying compared to the power in his hand. He trailed heat along her jaw and neck, to her collar bone...down, down, until he circled the mound of her breast.

All thoughts of slowing him evaporated. Yes, he was a stranger touching her private flesh, but for the first time, that was exciting—because, deep down, she realized she trusted him.

Moaning an invitation to continue, she closed her eyes.

His touch coiled up her breast toward the center. Sensation skittered in his fingers' wake, rumpling her skin with shivery goose bumps, furling her nipple tighter and tighter until he reached the peak—and thumbed it. She gasped at the jolt of pleasure. Gaze tight on her face, he flicked her nipple, thumb rasping softly, watching her reaction. Each flick showered her with electric sparks.

Bending again, he used his hot mouth to follow the path of his fingers, kissing warm and wet down her jaw and neck. His tongue flicked out to rasp against her sensitive flesh.

Annaliese whimpered, the sensations almost too much to handle.

"It's okay," Ransom murmured. Her eyes flew open. *He was still here.* Standing beside the bed, watching. In contrast to his soothing tones, her friend's sapphire eyes were bright.

Her insides flipped. Ransom was watching another man make love to her. She was furious with him; she adored him. *He didn't leave me.*

Then Jack's tongue reached her breast, breath scorching. His lips closed on her nipple, and he *sucked.*

Shrieking, Annaliese arched, forgetting Ransom, forgetting the pirate was a stranger, forgetting everything but this all-consuming *feeling*. Jack drew on her nipple, suckling deep.

As she trembled under him, his foot, bare of his conquistador boots, traced up her shin. Shifting his weight, he insinuated one leg between her calves and, still suckling, lowered himself—pinning her beneath him, his thigh wedged between her legs.

A flex of muscle spread her.

She gasped. His hot skin came into direct contact with her naked pussy, damp with desire, her clitoris raised. He flexed again, rubbing his strong, hair-covered thigh against her swollen clit.

She mewled.

He continued moving down, mouth following his hand. His thigh left her sex and she groaned at its absence...until his hand, big and strong, slid down her belly, ready to replaced it.

"May I?" His deep voice slid like black satin against her ears.

Panting robbed her of breath. Passion thickened her throat and tongue. Speech, was impossible. She could only nod.

It was enough.

He cupped her. His hand covered her pussy and then some. She moaned. He began to stroke, long, hard. She trembled. Heat seared her, increasing with every stroke.

He slid one finger inside her.

Need came to a head. She arched again, more violently.

Jack's hand began to rock and thrust, strong, regular. "I love how you feel," he murmured. "So hot. So wet. So ready."

Ready for what?

But he was moving down again, his finger withdrawing. This time she actively whimpered her protest.

Until he fastened onto her pussy with his mouth.

She shrieked. The sensations were coming too hard, too fast to keep up. Her body burned with need as her pussy spasmed under his hot mouth.

Tongue slapping, he worked her slit. She thrashed under him on the mattress, her legs caught under his weight.

Lust boiled up into a single desire—she had to suck on something, *now*. The need sang through her as Jack drew on her clit, sucking sounds coming from between her legs but also her own mouth.

"Want this?" Ransom offered his long, artistic finger.

Annaliese latched on, drawing on her friend like a Popsicle.

"Oh, fuck, *yeah*." Ransom's tenor was darker, deeper than she'd ever heard it. She slit eyes to see him eating her up with his gaze. "She's ready. Damn, she is *so* ready."

Jack gave her pussy a final tender kiss and rose to his knees, taking something from Ransom. His hands flashed as he tore open a foil packet. He rolled latex over his cock then positioned himself between her limp, wet thighs.

Watching him fit the head of his cock, sheathed in a condom, to her, she was surprised to realize she *ached* to receive him.

"Are you sure?" His whisper was taut with his own desire.

Was she sure? No. But she *needed*. Utterly without voice, she responded the only way she could, by curling her hips, pushing the head of him inside her.

He shuddered. "Fuck me. I'll take that as a yes." Rocking his hips, he withdrew slightly, and she moaned—until he drove forward with all the power that was in him.

"Yes!" She recovered speech in a sharp thrill as his first thrust filled her. Stretched her. She groaned to her pit...and tilted her hips so he could thrust again. "More. Deeper." A throaty, sensual voice emerged from her mouth, the seductress she'd longed to be.

He drove into her again. Shifting hands beside her head, he began thrusting, regular and strong, bold, fierce strokes as heavy and primal as the earth. He gazed down at her with his one eye, pirate's face drawn in a look of passion so beautiful, so compelling, her body responded directly. Dark, powerful orgasm built in her pelvis.

Triumph blazed in his eye. He'd seen her catch fire. His rhythm changed, grinding at the end of each thrust, friction and pressure billowing her flames into a bonfire. Passion burned through her, ready to explode, needing only one more push.

"Gotcha covered, punkin'." Ransom cupped her face, and his mouth found hers in a searing kiss.

Tasting Ransom, filled with Jack, she cried out, climaxing hard.

Jack thrust into her one last time, to the hilt, his shout blending with hers. His hot spurts sent her soaring.

Ransom's tongue, thrusting as deep as Jack's cock, made her explode anew.

Climax lit her brain, her soul. A nova of intense joy haloed around her, inside her. Feelings cascaded in colored lights behind her closed lids, red pleasure, yellow satisfaction, blue purity. White happiness.

Minutes or hours later, she came to herself, cooling but comforted by the heavy press of Jack's body, half-on, half-off. Ransom's mouth was gone but Jack's heartbeat was reassuringly strong and regular.

Muscles she never knew she had were relaxed, pliant. Her first words were a raspy, "Wow. Just...wow."

"Yeah, about that," Ransom said, tone as tight as a wound wire.

Chapter Seven

Ransom thought his cock was going to rupture. He looked down at himself, fly bulging so big that it was only his tailor-made zipper that kept him from being as exposed as the pirate.

He couldn't quite help the pained grunt which escaped instead.

Annaliese's lids fluttered up, gingerbread gaze locking with his. Sated. Confused. Beautiful.

Utterly relaxed, while he was so excited he was about to burst.

For the first time, he wasn't excited because of the risk. His heart beat faster because Annaliese had had *fun*. He truly loved seeing her taking her pleasure.

An idea nudged him.

He'd held back on having sex with her, not because he didn't *want* her, but because he didn't want to *hurt* her. Because withdrawn, shrinking-from-risk Annaliese was so fragile.

But a different Annaliese had sucked on his finger with such abandon. A new, fearless woman met Jack thrust for thrust on this bed. This Annie had actually enjoyed herself.

And if she'd enjoyed the mild risk of sex with a new man—which jacked Ransom's cock even fatter, until it was fucking painful—maybe she was even ready for sex with him.

He wanted her so badly he was about to explode. But even now he held back, asking himself if lovemaking would truly be okay. He couldn't hurt Annaliese. Because he loved her, he had to make absolutely sure she wouldn't regret their making love

Good fuck. I'm not thinking in terms of sex or screwing or fucking. I'm thinking of making love.

Maybe, after all this time, he could do it. Maybe he could finally become the man she needed.

Jack released a deep, "*Mmm.*"

Ah hell. Didn't matter if Ransom could or couldn't be the man she needed. He'd watched her and the pirate move together, answering, then *anticipating* each other's desires. They'd clicked at the most basic level there was.

But while Jack was obviously the man for her, Ransom still held Annie's heart. She would never give Jack a real chance, unless Ransom showed her how it would be with him.

He almost had to give her an orgasm too, so she'd be able to compare. Know for sure.

So make love to her. If, after, she still wanted *him,* he'd offer to share his life with her. If she wanted the pirate, he'd cede with a happy face—and a broken heart.

He pasted on a roguish grin. "Jack. Want to give her another orgasm?"

The other man gave him a sharp look. "Are you kidding? She's not ready." But the yearning in his dark eye told the entire story.

"She will be. Follow my lead."

Annaliese roused. "Ransom? What are you doing?"

"Shh, punkin'. It'll be good. You'll see." Whether she picked the pirate or not, Ransom was confident enough in his own abilities that he could at least show her a good time. He stripped off his clothes, unzipping his pants last. His cock leaped out, bobbing eagerly.

Annaliese sucked in a breath, wide eyes dropping to his erection.

Yeah. After seeing the pirate's plank, he'd wondered if she'd still be impressed, but now his jaw kicked up in pride.

Meanwhile, Jack had rolled to one side to strip off his used condom, his own cock filling and thickening with renewed interest.

If this was half as exciting as Ransom imagined, the pirate would be spurting again in no time.

He put a hand on Jack's back to guide him into position between Annaliese's glistening thighs and got the shock of his life. The man was pure, hard muscle, his flank like curved polished ironwood. Unbidden, Ransom's hand slid down the contours to the man's buttock, roped concentrated power. It was all he could do not to knead, all he could do not to try an experimental slap.

The pirate cut him a dark glare, one black eyebrow arched. "You do and you'll regret it."

Ransom smirked and gave his glutes a buddy pat anyway.

The pirate, too fast to counter, grabbed Ransom by the nape and pinned him to the bed, hunched over Annaliese.

Ransom's blood spiked with adrenaline, but his belly exploded in desire. The man was immensely strong. Immensely dangerous.

More dangerous and exciting than any extreme sport Ransom had ever attempted to conquer.

Am I really thinking about trying to conquer the pirate? It held its own fascination, but besides the niggling feeling that he *couldn't,* he didn't want to piss the man off right now. Annaliese wouldn't have fun if Jack throttled him. Not to mention the best adrenaline rush of Ransom's life would be wasted.

He waved a hand of truce in the air. "Peace."

Jack let him up, his single eye narrowed, cautious. Wary.

Ransom's blood juiced. He'd have to seduce, not simply Annaliese, but a recalcitrant pirate.

Well, yeah. He was always up for a challenge.

The best way to start a seduction was chocolate, caresses, and kisses. No chocolate here, so that left the second two.

"Annaliese, sit up." Ransom helped her, sliding behind her on the bed. "Now, I'm only going to touch your neck. No worries, right?"

"Right?" She echoed it as a question, her gingerbread eyes twitching toward him.

"No worries," he repeated firmly, underlining how nonthreatening he was by brushing his knuckles along her neck, tendon stretched from her turned head. The taut cord relaxed under his tender caress, her neck arching into a graceful curve, her head beginning to loll.

When she was relaxed enough to enjoy the next step, Ransom nodded to the other man on the bed.

Jack faced Annaliese and Ransom's doubled bodies. Expecting Jack would start by cupping her breasts, Ransom was surprised and delighted when the pirate skimmed his fingertips along her face, tracing her cheek to the curl of her nostril, from there brushing a thumb across her sensitive mouth.

The man's light touch brought a soft smile to her lips.

Suddenly Ransom had to taste them. He wasn't sure if he meant her lips or the pirate's fingers or both.

He wrapped one arm around Annaliese's waist and cinched in behind her, his chest to her spine, his trailing leg framing her left hip and thigh. Her head was already turned. A tap on her chin raised it, tipping her head back, until her lips were right under his, her breath sweet in his nostrils. Her languorous lids slit open with mild curiosity. Under his arm, her body was relaxed and warm, perfect.

He bent and kissed her. Sugar-sweet mouth and breath, with a salty hint left behind from the pirate's caress. More than perfect.

Almost automatically, the tip of his tongue came out for a lick.

She gave a surprised laugh. Her lids lifted, and she rewarded him with her sweet smile, eyes gently twinkling.

He fell in and drowned. *Annaliese is enjoying herself—with me.* It seemed he'd been waiting for that look his whole life. Amazement and joy was a helium balloon in his chest. As good as—no, *better* than the best adrenaline rush in his life.

The realization stunned him.

"Ransom?" Annie's soft voice called him back to the program.

He nodded at Jack. "Now you." *If the pirate only knew what I'm planning...*

Maybe the man had gotten turned on watching Ransom plunder Annaliese's luscious lips. Maybe he was just that powerfully direct.

The pirate seized her mouth, jaw working, lots of tongue.

Ransom's cock exploded. He barely resisted the urge to join in, to feel that dark power in his own mouth.

But he could only stand so much torment. "Now me." Ransom pushed the other man's head to the side and kissed Annaliese again. She was panting by now. He swiped his tongue into her mouth.

Tasted raw, dark male mingling with the female nectar.

Oh yeah. More of this. Much, *much* more of exactly this.

"Now you." Ransom lifted his head, leaving less room this time for Jack's cliff of a jaw to wedge in. He could feel the other man's heat, practically taste his mouth devouring Annaliese.

Now me, Ransom thought, but he didn't say it out loud. He simply shimmed his face beside Jack's and kissed the exposed corner of Annaliese's lips—damn, the pirate had a big mouth—licking to encourage her to open farther.

Her jaw dropped as far as possible. He darted his tongue past the corner, inside her mouth...where Jack's was commanding her, thrusting deep.

Their tongues met.

Oh yeah. A long slide of sexual need shivered through Ransom's body as the three of them began to kiss. Whose tongue, whose mouth, who was sucking at whose lips? Sweet and dark swirled and mingled. It was fucking awesome.

Then Jack's powerful arms came around Annaliese...and since Ransom was seamed with her body, those pirate's arms claimed him too. Jack pulled both of them to his chest, and with a groan, kissed both in earnest.

Annaliese gave a little cry. Ransom recognized she was close to being overwhelmed.

But that also meant she was at the edge of the best time of her life.

Jack, perhaps not realizing that, started to back off.

With a firm hug, Ransom reassured her that he was still here, would stay with her. Then he slid one arm around Jack's waist, pulling him back, tighter, into the threesome.

The contrast slammed through Ransom. The man's body was satin over boulders, the woman's silky soft. Ransom's cock raged and throbbed, needing to plunge into dark and wet and hot *now*.

He was so aroused he wanted to shout with it.

Under his hand, the pirate's flank bunched. He'd bent, dropping his head to Annaliese's breast.

Leaving the other to Ransom. He shifted sideways and down to touch a tongue to the creamy globe.

Jack began to suckle. Annaliese's whimpers changed to delighted little mews, shooting fiery bolts of pleasure through Ransom. *Good idea.* Ransom licked to Annaliese's other nipple, and sucked it into his mouth.

Listening to the pirate's sucks, Ransom began to suckle her in tandem.

She cried out, arching into the pair of them, into their mouths. Her delighted moans were music to his ears. She was almost ready for his own oral loving.

He was going to rock her world, not because he was in competition with the pirate, though he was, but because Annaliese deserved it.

Slowly, he petted down her belly to her mound. Slid a finger into the shallow dent that was the start of her sweet little slit. Went exploring...

His finger skidded down the nose of her clit. She wasn't simply wet, she was drenched, and her clit was swollen so big and hard it was like a marble.

She wasn't almost ready. She was beyond ready.

Ransom nearly lost it all over the spread. He had to pant hard a few seconds to control himself.

Then, shifting half off the bed, he eased her onto her back. Jack followed her down, mouth still hot on her nipple, as if he couldn't bear to leave such heaven.

Ransom's intent was other manna. He nudged the other man to her far side, to give him free access to her pussy. But he started slow. Kissing her middle, licking the small hairs down her belly to her the top of her mound—which he gave a big wet kiss.

She made a little mew of protest and began to struggle to her elbows.

Ransom lifted his gaze, met Jack's eye. The pirate nodded. Jack raised himself to his knees beside her, seized her nipples between thumbs and forefingers, and distracted her with a kiss so hot, Ransom's tongue swelled.

Well, good. Swollen and wet. Perfect for what he was about to do.

He crawled between her legs and went down on her.

She thrashed under his mouth. He tasted her and Jack and doubled his eagerness, slapping his tongue and sucking and kissing. Her mews changed to groans, deep, from her belly. When her pussy spasmed under his mouth, he glanced up to see her face.

Jack had lifted his head to watch Ransom pleasure her. Without the pirate's mouth kissing her, she was making the cute little sucking sounds she'd made before. Then, Ransom had given her his finger, unable to resist. He knew Jack would be unable to resist putting something in her hot mouth too.

Even so, when the man straddled her head, Ransom nearly ruptured. Before the pirate's big body blocked his view, Ransom saw Annaliese's eyes wide open on the pirate, a little frightened but also a lot eager.

From above, Jack slid his monster erection between her pretty lips.

Then Ransom could only see Jack's back, undulating. Hips rolling. Buttocks pushing in and out like a breathing creature.

Fuck, that was hot. So hot, Ransom was about to burst.

But not without taking Annaliese with him.

He rolled on a condom, slid his arms under her legs and raised her knees. Then he skewered her dripping pussy.

She screamed. Even muffled by Jack's driving cock, her pleasure was the sweetest thing he'd ever heard.

After that he couldn't hold back. He rode her hard, ripping stroke after stroke into her swollen, wet channel. He buried himself over and over into her soft, spasming flesh, until he finally buried himself so deep it felt as if he'd touched her soul.

She cried out, and her pussy gave a hard clench around his cock. The pirate gave a hoarse, guttural shout, and came too.

Male and female voices twined in Ransom's ears, joining with the tight need in his body and twisting it to the limit.

Breaking it wide open.

His first spurt was so hard, it felt like it blew his balls off. With the scent of Jack and Annaliese and raw pleasure in his nostrils, he climaxed, soaring from the highest peak in his life. He sailed like a falcon spreading wings from a cliff, like a skier riding chop.

The next contraction hit, sending him farther. And the next, the next next...it went on and on, and if he weren't only human, he felt like it could have gone on forever.

But he was human and eventually sank back into his body, his hearing returning to the rasp of his breath in his ears, the thud of his hammering heart.

God. That sex had been the best of his life.

Although, could he really call it that? Sex? With Annaliese, everything that had happened was more beautiful and rewarding than he'd expected.

And with Jack, everything was darker, harder, more electrifying.

Annaliese filled his heart—but Jack thrilled his soul.

Ransom fell onto the mattress beside the other two, utterly destroyed by the realization.

So he wasn't able to do a thing when Jack got off the bed, adjusted his pouch to cover himself, snatched up his boots and strode out the door.

Chapter Eight

"Jack, wait." The words caught in Annaliese's throat and her voice cracked, calling after the amazing, infuriating, fantastically sexy pirate. Her mouth was sore too, an unfamiliar but good ache from stubbled kisses and the absolute necessity of sucking on fingers and cocks.

The rest of her body felt clean, new. Absolutely at peace, so welcome after years of the low-grade fever she'd carried for Ransom.

But now she wanted Jack, too.

A slam followed her hoarse shout. He was already out the bedroom door. *Damn it*.

She leaped to her feet...or tried to. The rest of her body suddenly revealed itself to be as cranky as her mouth.

Thrashing sore muscles, she managed to worm to the edge of the mattress and stumbled off the bed to her feet. Her crotch was sore too, the same kind of happy, well-used sore as her muscles and mouth.

She'd just pleasured, and been pleasured by, two men. Unbelievably risky and outrageously improper—and the best time she'd ever had.

"Jack, please? Come back." She called as loud as she could as she tottered toward the closed door. Making it to the door, she grabbed the knob, about to throw it open and dash out after the pirate.

The old hesitation came back.

She was nude. What if it Jack was long gone? What if other party guests were in the hallway, saw her burst out naked, and laughed?

What if they were a slew of gorgeous women wanting to wish Ransom a happier birthday than she ever could?

She glanced back at the bed. Ransom lay on the mattress, raised on his elbows, blinking. For a moment she forgot the parade of women. Today, he'd had sex with *her*. Not just sex, but amazing sex. Sex so deep, it connected with her soul—and his.

A shiver of pleasure threaded her. Ransom had made love to her, and by the look on his face, it had touched his soul too.

No parade of women could have given him that.

Ransom started frowning, but his gaze was still a bit befuddled, as if he was so blown away by what the three of them had done on that mattress that he couldn't quite grasp what the closed door meant.

But he knew something was wrong.

A darkness in her chest echoed that something *was* wrong. Jack was gone.

The darkness immediately clouded her happiness. Ransom had made love to her...and *Jack.*

The three of them had touched each other. Without Jack, Ransom might go right back to being only her friend.

Her soul shriveled.

No. Not going back, especially not to that platonic friend-zone.

She had to risk the corridor.

Open that door and call Jack back. She grasped the knob more firmly and, with a deep breath for courage, threw open the door and shouted his name with everything inside her. "Jack!"

He leaned against the opposite wall, putting on his second boot, the first already on. Without looking from his task, he rapped out, "What." His tone was flat.

"Don't go. We need to talk."

He looked up then. Pain was in his gaze, and a bare spark of hope that was already drowning. "There's nothing to talk about."

"How can you say that?"

He got his boot on and stamped it onto the floor. "Annaliese, you might have been the one for me. But..."

He paused, and that *might have been* killed her heart. She *saw* the pain submerge the last of his hope. She whispered, "But...?"

"But I can see you love Ransom."

At the name, without meaning to, she glanced back at her friend. He was finally rousing, sitting up.

A soft sound of pain came from Jack, as if she'd just proved who she loved more.

Anguish flooding her, she immediately gave the pirate her complete attention. "Yes, I love him. I'm so sorry." She swallowed hard. The agony on Jack's face made her die a little. She'd felt what he was going through, had felt it each time Ransom drifted off with another gorgeous female. "If it's any consolation, he doesn't love me."

"He doesn't love anybody or anything."

Jack's angry snarl told her he was sticking up for her more than he was dissing Ransom. She said, "He loves excitement. He craves the adrenaline rush."

"Doesn't matter *why*." Jack pushed off from the wall, his feet and shoulders already turned to stride off. Walk out of her life forever. "Doesn't change anything."

Her stomach plummeted, her chest filled with ice. "Don't go. *Please*. I-I need you too."

"No. You need *him* to step up and do right by you." Jack frowned, his head coming around, gaze narrowed past her, as if he could see into the bedroom. "Dipshit." He shook his head and swung away.

Ready to take those few long strides and be gone. Annaliese's heart plunged, and her eyes filled with liquid fire.

Then Jack swore, spun on one foot and barreled toward her. She was so surprised she stood frozen, blinking. His big body displaced her like a semi passing a bike as he swept back into the room.

He hasn't gone yet. Heart leaping, she followed him inside, clicked the door shut behind her, and locked it, as if that would keep Jack with them forever.

Her actions surprised her. She loved Ransom, but the pirate had revealed himself as astute and noble, gentle yet powerful. He was the man maybe she should have loved.

But one thing was clear. Even though her heart still belonged to Ransom, she'd come to care deeply about Jack too.

As Annaliese turned to say something of the sort, Jack, his naked shoulders hunched like a linebacker, strode to the bed—and he punched Ransom in the arm.

"Grow the fuck up."

"Ow." Ransom rubbed the spot. "You pirates pack quite a wallop." He grinned at the other man. "Kind of a turn on."

"Ass." But Jack rolled amused eyes in return. "Seriously. You need to be the man she needs."

"I know." Ransom's words were sober, genuine, and his always-ready grin faded. "Believe me, I've tried. I do love her."

She gaped. She'd never heard him utter those words before, not as anything more than a big brother teasing his kid sister.

But even she could tell this time Ransom meant something far more adult.

This was a side of him Annaliese had never seen. She'd never been able to reach his sober, mature self, but somehow Jack had found it and brought it out.

Jack, again. Making them both better people.

"Just grow the fuck up." Flipping his pirate's patch up on his head, Jack nailed Ransom with both eyes in a glare so narrow Annaliese winced, feeling it clear across the room.

"I've *tried*." Ransom rose to his feet and matched Jack's anger with his own, chest to chest. "Don't you think I've tried? Don't you think I've worked to extinguish the wild side of me, to become the man she needs—no, more, the man she *deserves?*" As if his emotions drove him, Ransom poked Jack in the chest. "That should be *you*."

"Maybe it should be," Jack growled, muscles tense. "But it's not. It's you." He poked Ransom back, apparently no harder, but his strength was such that her friend went reeling, falling back onto the bed.

Ransom, never one to stand for physical insult, clambered onto his elbows, face contorted with dark anger. "How dare you—"

"You poked me first." Jack ratcheted his own glare up a notch, and she could see a muscle in his jaw whiten.

"You poked me harder." Ransom regained his feet, not jumping this time but sliding up, cautious, muscles loose and relaxed—ready to fight.

Jack's eyes went to narrow slits. "I did not poke you harder—"

"Wait!" Annaliese hurried to the men before they could escalate any more. She touched Jack's biceps—the muscle was clenched and rock hard. "Jack, please." She turned to Ransom and petted her other hand down his arm. Not as bulging a biceps as Jack, but no less tense. Neither looked at her, their glares locked.

The energy between them so strong a force it was almost visible.

And Annaliese had an idea.

It was a risk. She'd let the men take charge of the sex, but now it was her turn to organize. To lead.

Time for her to step up.

So what if it was risky? If they were to have any chance at happiness, it was her turn to make the sacrifice. Not only give up her new job on the other coast, but bare a side of herself she'd just found and hardly knew how to handle. The potential for pain was great.

But if these two agreed, she'd gain so much more.

"Jack, go sit down. There." She pointed at a chair facing the bed but several running steps away.

Jack, with one final glare, spun and stomped two long strides to sit, arms folded across his bulky chest.

One running step then. She'd stand between. It would be enough. It had to be.

"Ransom, you did start this." When he opened his mouth to object, she shut him down with a gentle palm to the lips. "When you told me to have sex with Jack."

He moved his mouth under her palm. She lifted her hand.

"I admit it," he said. "But didn't you enjoy it?"

"Almost more than anything in the world."

Her friend's shoulder's relaxed at that, and he tipped her a smile. "Good. I'm glad."

"Almost," she repeated.

Ransom's smile faded, and Jack frowned.

"I enjoyed the three of us together more."

"The sex was pretty hot," Ransom admitted, smile springing back brighter.

"It was more than sex," Jack rumbled. "At least for me."

"Which is why you have to stay," she said to him. "It was more than sex for me, too."

"Not for everyone." Jack lurched to his feet with a glare at Ransom. "Which is why I have to go."

As he began to turn toward the door, Annaliese exchanged a glance with Ransom, begging him wordlessly to help.

For a breathless moment, he only frowned. Then his eyes widened. He got it.

Yet as Jack took the first step away from her, from *them,* Ransom hesitated.

His blond head dropped, and slowly shook.

Sweet lord. Ransom was afraid.

Her heart went out to him. She understood. She had felt that fear before throwing open the door to call after Jack, naked to the world and not knowing what she'd find.

The doorknob jangled. Jack had discovered it was locked.

Their one chance at happiness, her last chance. But Ransom couldn't do it. Ransom, who was afraid of nothing, was afraid of this. Intimacy. Caring too much.

She hurt for him, but her heart, when it crumpled, died a little for them all. Clenching her eyelids, a single tear threaded hot down her cheek. Her breath hurt, and she pressed it out, trying to purge the pain with it, but it wouldn't go around the lump in her throat.

"Annie?"

She opened her eyes. Ransom searched her face, rare uncertainty touching his expression.

Clicks behind her told her Jack was fiddling with the lock. In another moment he'd be gone.

Her throat was too swollen for words. She gave Ransom a watery smile, trying to tell him that she understood. That she still loved him.

Behind her came the sound of the knob turning, the latch pulling back. She glanced over her shoulder to see Jack throw the door open.

She turned around, letting her head and shoulders droop, not having the stomach to watch her pirate leave.

"Damn it," Ransom muttered. Then he raised his voice. "So that's it, huh? She doesn't love you after an hour, so you're just giving up?"

Annaliese blinked and straightened in surprise. Hesitantly, she twisted to see Jack.

He glared over his broad shoulder. Snarled, "What the hell is that supposed to mean?"

She suddenly felt in the way. She stepped back, clearing the line between the two men.

"Look, I get it." Ransom held up his hands in the V of a shrug so familiar to her. "I'm scared too."

She stopped breathing.

"I'm not scared." Jack's throat must've been tight because the words sounded almost grated. "I'm leaving because she loves *you*. Not me."

"Yes, she loves me." Ransom laughed, no humor in it. "What a bunch of fools we are. Annaliese saw it first. You're attracted to her, she loves me...and *I* love the rush a man like you provides. Don't you see? We fit like three puzzle pieces."

Annaliese's breath came back in a rush.

Her best friend, the boy of her heart. On the same page with her, understanding her. Only this time he not only understood—and he was scared too but right beside her on that high dive, taking the plunge. Leaping off the tire swing with her into the lake.

Both of them happily drowning.

This chance to be with their pirate was worth it.

"What are you suggesting?" Jack's frown had deepened, but he came back into the room and slowly shut the door.

"We had a satisfying sexual encounter, right?"

"Right."

"Why not grow it into more? Or at least try. Grow it into a...I don't know, what is it you want? A lifelong emotionally satisfying thing?"

"You've got a real way with words, Blondie."

An echo of Ransom's old grin came back. "Okay, maybe we can just take it a day at a time. But stay. At the very least, it'll give you time to get to know Annie better. Who knows? Maybe she'll fall out of love with me and in love with you." A grimace flashed across his aristocratic features.

"Maybe." Jack's frown echoed the pain in Ransom's. "But maybe not. Maybe she'll never stop loving you."

"Maybe not," Annaliese said. Time to risk it all. She walked firmly to Jack and rested her palm on his chest. "But maybe I'll fall in love with both of you, had you considered that?"

Jack blinked. "No, I hadn't." His gaze dropped to her hand, touching his skin, then rose to search her face. "Maybe." Frowning, his gaze rose, dark eye staring over her head as if the future was written on the far wall.

She held her breath.

"I guess for even a possible future with you...I could try."

Her breath came back and she rewarded him with a big smile. Then she held her other hand toward her friend. "Ransom? For the a possible future with you...I'll try more excitement."

"All *right*." He leaped to his feet, glided over, and took her hand. Answering her smile with his grin crackling with friendship and support, love and joy, he pressed her palm to his own chest.

Then he raised his free hand to Jack. "For a future with you...ah hell. It'll be a lot of work. But I'm willing to try if you are."

She turned her gaze to Jack too.

He was staring at Ransom. She couldn't tell what was going on behind his pirate's eyes.

Her heart stuttered.

Then Jack gave a shrug. "Annaliese sees *something* in you." He took Ransom's hand and slapped it to the other side of his chest before grabbing both their shoulders, one in each hand. "Maybe I could give you a chance too."

Her heart burst with joy.

*   *   *

Frowning, Annaliese considered where the next item should go.

Not that she had to move it. She sipped a glass of champagne, sitting on the bedroom bench. They'd bought an apartment together, and today they were moving in, another step toward their future.

"Can you hurry up, Annie?" Ransom complained. "This dresser is heavy."

"What can I say? It's antique. Things were built better back in the day." Annaliese considered Jack, on the other side of the dresser. He looked like Colossus, as if he could stand there holding the heavy thing forever. "It was my grandmother's."

"Three strikes for Granny," Ransom muttered.

"All right, over there." Annaliese relented with a grin. It was exciting to flirt...well, exciting to flirt with two men she knew loved her. "Put it between your dresser and Jack's."

The men eased the piece between the other two already in the spacious master bedroom.

"Perfect fit." Jack nudged the furniture square. He flashed Annaliese a smile. "As perfect as we are."

Ransom, with an impish grin Annaliese recognized said, "Right you are, pirate."

Before she could warn Jack, Ransom raised his hand and smacked him on the bottom, immediately dancing back.

Jack spun with a roar. He lunged forward, long muscular arms grabbing for Ransom.

Annaliese had to laugh at the way Ransom's eyes widened. He'd thought he'd put enough space between them? That miscalculation got him picked up and tossed onto the king-size bed.

Jack leaped up behind him and efficiently put Ransom face-first into the mattress. "You earned this." He smacked Ransom on the behind—twice. Two good smacks that had Annaliese squirming.

"Ow," Ransom said, but his butt was wiggling for another.

Jack stifled a smile and turned to Annaliese. "Your turn."

"It certainly is." She set down her glass. It was still so new to her, and exciting.

For the first time in her life, she couldn't wait to play.

About the Author

Remi Bond loves the spark that brings two (or three or four or more) people together, the love that makes them better human beings, and the drive and work that, despite life's difficulties, keeps them together.

Let's play!

Remi's online and would love to hear from you!

Website http://www.remibond.com/

Email: remi@remibond.com

Newsletter signup http://www.remibond.com/

Remi Bond

Turn the page for a special preview of *The Spy Makes Three* by Remi Bond, coming soon, and teasers and excerpts from Leap Year story *Chasing Dreams* by S. L. Carpenter, and April Fools For Love stories *Cin Wikkid* by Mary Hughes, *Bottled Up* by Roxy Mews, *Toy Story* by S.L. Carpenter and *Must Love Menage* by Kaleigh Malcolm, now available in ebook.

The Spy Makes Three
© 2016 Remi Bond

Carter and Kaylee Anderson aren't unhappy with their lives, exactly. But by their third anniversary they feel there ought to be more to life. A romantic getaway promises to spice things up.

Drinking in a seedy bar, they don't recognize Jackson Brand, the sexy nerd the couple knew in high school, because he's grown up tall, dark and dangerous. He's a spy on a mission, but his cover is about to be blown.

He hides out in the couple's room to solve the problem, never dreaming he's trading one tricky predicament for a much bigger pair.

Enjoy the following excerpt from *The Spy Makes Three*:

Kaylee Anderson tipped the second pitcher of lime beer, *tinking* it unsteadily against her glass as she poured her refill. "It's not that I hate my job. It's just so predictable."

"Sure. It's steady. That's one of the reasons you took it." Carter, her husband of three years, glanced at his phone, displaying a notepad app. "See? It's in the plus column."

"Yes, but...well, predictable was good in the beginning, but now it seems dead end." She drank her beer, letting the bright flavor wash down her throat. Nearby, short-skirted barmaids threaded the crowded barroom, plunking cheap tappers on tables ringed by scruffy men sweating over their poker cards. Along one wall, a line of backs hunched over solitary beers and whiskeys.

"I just have this feeling here—" she touched her breastbone, "—that there's supposed to be more to work. More to life." She set her glass down with a rueful smile. "Look at me, talking work on our anniversary. We got out of town to spice things up, to get away from work."

"Kaylee." Carter took her hands. His were warm and comforting. "Whenever you need me, wherever, I'm here for you. Especially on our anniversary."

She smiled into his intense blue eyes and brushed back a strand of his dark hair. She loved him as much for that dependable strength as for his sinewy build and classically handsome features. He held her eyes with the serious focus that he brought to everything he did, including making love.

Which, hopefully, they would do soon.

He caught the heated look in her eye and gave her a simmering smile in return. "Let's finish this pitcher and head up." He topped off her glass before pouring the last of the pitcher into his. A gentleman too. She was lucky to have found him.

"Thanks Carter, I appreciate your listening. It's not like you're any happier at your architectural firm."

Carter shrugged. "I'm not unhappy."

"But not happy either." She sighed, wondering if it was the beer making her maudlin. "Oh, enough of this. It's our anniversary. Leave the beer. Let's go upstairs and get kinky."

"The red nightie?" Carter's smile turned wicked. "That's definitely not boring."

"And the toy we bought." Kaylee knocked back the rest of her beer and stood. "Our first vibrator. Have you ever used one?"

Carter threw a tip on the table and rose too. "No, but that'll be part of the fun." He raised his eyebrows at her. "An adventure."

She laughed. "Our first adventure." Still smiling, she took his hand and led him, weaving a bit, past the long bar with its row of backs. "This anniversary, we add spice to our life." She flipped to face him as she started to skip.

And crashed into a bad-smelling, over-stuffed shirt of a stocky man, knocking off his dull red sport cap.

She bounced off and would have fallen—but for a strong hand lancing from the row of backs at the bar. A masculine hand, gripping her arm firmly, set her aright.

Her husband wasn't so lucky.

The stocky man stumbled and fell heavily against Carter. Limbs tangled and they went down, hitting the floor with an audible whump.

"Hey, look." A mean-looking man sneered at the stocky guy now squashing her husband. He spoke to a pair of men, all three wearing the same dull red sport caps. "Lou's got a pretty boyfriend. You gonna do it on the floor, Lou?"

"What the hell?" Lou huffed to his feet, a snarl on his face. "He hit me, the asshole."

Carter rolled awkwardly to hands and knees. His face was pale. He didn't answer immediately, his eyes taking in the room. Kaylee became aware of all the people staring at them. Carter said, "I guess we were both 'a hit'. Ba-dum-bum."

Her husband's dry sense of humor, which kicked in under stress, was unfortunately timed. The stocky man grabbed Carter's collar and jerked him to his feet. Carter's face went dead white.

"You asshole. Nobody hits me and gets away with it." Lou shifted his hold on Carter's collar, winching it tighter. The other three cheered him on.

The man was all beer belly, body hair and toxic attitude. His friends seemed just as nasty. Kaylee shot an anxious glance around the barroom. Surely there was a bouncer or bartender to keep control. Someone.

Eyes watched avidly, but the way spectators did at a disaster. These people wouldn't get involved.

Carter gasped for air. "Look, I'm sorry."

"You're gonna be sorrier." Lou shook a fist in Carter's face.

"Please." Kaylee put a trembling hand on Lou's arm. "Don't hurt Carter. It's not his fault—"

"Fuck that." The stocky man shoved her. "And fuck you."

She stumbled, barely caught herself against a rock-hard wall.

A warm wall, with a deep voice that said, "Excuse me."

A firm hand, the same masculine hand that had first steadied her, moved Kaylee gently aside. She shivered as a tall shadow glided past her, leaving the impression of dark and dangerous strength and the scent of leather and soap in its wake.

The shadow towered over Lou. "You'll want to let him go."

Chasing Dreams
© 2016 S.L. Carpenter

Leap Year

Michelle has reached a crossroads in her life just as the year offers her an extra day – February 29th. Walking away from an empty relationship and striking out on a new path is reviving feelings—both scary and wonderful. A train trip home offers time to think about her future, and what the Leap Year might bring. It also offers her a good looking drunk, passed out in her sleeping compartment.

Josh is mortified that he crashed in the wrong compartment, but fascinated by the woman who let him sleep and even covered him with a blanket. Their meeting seems pre-destined, as does the passion sparking between them.

But they both have pasts, and sometimes the past can leave a long shadow across the future. Michelle and Josh will have to come to terms with where they've been before they can really set off on the ultimate adventure...chasing their dreams.

Enjoy the following excerpt from *Chasing Dreams*:

Struggling with feelings and the awkward uncertain situation, they walked back to her compartment. Josh leaned down and kissed Michelle. She placed her hand on his neck and let her lips move against his. God, he was so hot. Inside she was on fire, but she had to contain it.

"Goodnight, Josh, thank you for a wonderful evening."

"You sure? I mean I could..."

Michelle stopped him from continuing. "Let's not ruin this with a torrid night of incredible, hot, passionate, earth shattering sex."

"Yeah, that would really be a bad thing," he sighed, looking down at her.

He kissed her forehead then raised her face with his hands and kissed her lips. His hands lowered along her sides, brushing the sensitive skin aside her breast.

"Mmm, oh yes," she murmured.

Her hands found his waist and her knees weakened at the affectionate way he kissed her. Her mouth dropped open and she lifted her head back when Josh blew hot air gently into her ear and squeezed her ass. She almost succumbed to his advances because she was already wet in anticipation for him.

"Josh, I c-c-can't." She hesitated before pushing him back. "I can't just jump into another relationship like this. It's too soon."

Looking down, Josh nodded but was obviously disappointed. He walked to his room and waved at Michelle but didn't turn towards her because his hard-on was making his pants poke out.

Michelle was torn. What should she do?

A fairytale romance meets 4G.

Cin Wikkid
© 2016 Mary Hughes

April Fools For Love

THE WRONGED DAUGHTER
Cinderella hungers to escape from under Widow Wikkid's grinding thumb. But to snare a plum job at Prince Industries, Cin desperately needs her degree, and she can't wrap her mind around tax accounting.

Then scarred but sexy Rafe Montoya ignites her imagination with his brilliant tutoring—and, as they work together in his cozy apartment, he sets her body on fire. She thinks he's the one for her, until he starts pushing her to attend Gideon Prince's marriage-mart ball.

THE HANDSOME PRINCE
Rafe is really Gideon Prince, head of Prince Industries. He must name his bride by his April first birthday or suffer the loss of his family fortune.

Rumors say he's still single because women love his money and looks, not him. Is he lonely or just another duplicitous tycoon?

THE GLASS SLIPPER TEST

Hopefuls flock to Prince's birthday ball, but only the woman who is kind, wise, and generous will win his heart. Is it Cin, or will her stepmother, as she always does, snatch the prize for her own daughters?

And on the night of the ball, when Cin discovers Rafe's true identity, can she even accept his final test?

Warning: Rags-to-riches fairytale meets the texting generation. Stepsisters who are a blush-brush shy of a full makeup set, and a ball gown built like a tank. Contains material intended for mature audiences. Reader discretion advised.

Enjoy the following excerpt from *Cin Wikkid*:

Rafe watched her over the rim of his coffee mug, cobalt eyes twinkling.

Hesitantly, Cinderella told him about the mock hearing. "Is that something you can teach me?"

"Ye-es. Probably." He frowned, thoughtfully. "How long do we have?"

"Until the beginning of April."

"Then definitely yes. Though, it will take some pretty intense work one-on-one." One black brow raised, a challenge. "Are you up for it?"

"I'm not afraid of hard work. Are *you* up for it?" Daringly, she raised both brows in return challenge.

The right corner of his mouth went up, on the scarred side, crinkling his skin and giving his grin a rakish, devil-may-care look. "Hours of intense work, one-on-one, with you? Oh, yeah. I'm up for it."

The way he purred "*up* for it" implied things beyond study. Physical things. Cin's stomach swooped and her heart pattered rapidly in response.

Then his eyes dropped to her mouth and heated.

Her whole body went *boom*.

She trembled, her heart pounding, her breath sawing in and out, on the cusp of bright truth. Her stepsiblings' hatred had taught her to cover herself in bad makeup and baggy clothes and work, the contemporary version of sacks and ashes. But Rafe, looking at her like that...as if he not only was attracted to her but was on *fire*...God. She wanted to tear off her rags and *shine*.

A clogged drain. A pretend plumber. An April Fool's Day to remember.

Bottled Up

April Fools For Love

Good looks don't last forever, and neither do modeling careers. When Nate's time in the sun ends, he goes back to school. Trouble is, in order to pay for his last semester he's going to need to get naked.

When a four month modeling contract took Nate Dallas on an adventure around the world, he was too young to realize he was an idiot to leave his Blue-eyed Betty behind. After one night of passion he let her love letters fade in his pocket instead of fighting for a trip home.

Betty Townsend never forgot about Nate. He'd sent her the world in envelopes filled with sea shells and sand. She saw stars when he kissed her under a sparkling spotlight on stage. And she felt her heart break when he never returned to her.

When Nate shows up at Betty's door, big wrench in hand, she can't believe her first love is the one her friend hired to fix the sink.

Once Nate recognizes Betty, stripping is out of the question. So is leaving. He can't throw this chance away. The heat between them is undeniable, but when Betty finds out her first love is covered in glitter down to his g-string, do they stand a chance at rekindling the love that never really burned out? Or will fate make fools out of them again?

Enjoy the following excerpt from *Bottled Up*:

Her brain had fried the second she'd realized it was Nate. She'd completely forgotten about the glossy paper with his oily pecs on it hanging over the frozen foods section of her home. The ad was an oldie, but a goodie, and the black sand he was standing on filled one of her bottles. The vitamin supplement wasn't the reason the VitaBoost ad was pinned up with a magnet. It was a memory.

Nate was damn near naked and holding a huge barbell in front of his...

A laugh came from the kitchen.

"Ang, I gotta go."

Her friend was sputtering as she ended the call, but it was Betty who was stumbling for words when she walked into the kitchen and found Nate holding the picture of himself.

He cocked his eyebrow at her, and a dimple popped on his left cheek. It was something she'd fantasized about endlessly. But not while he was holding up proof she'd been pining for him after all this time.

"I didn't even think they printed this anymore."

They didn't. She'd found an old magazine at a half price book store and snatched it up when she'd seen his face smoldering out at her.

"This is really embarrassing. It was a motivation pic for me," she lied. "I'm on a diet...and...could I have that back?" She reached for the magazine page and he pulled it behind his body at an angle that she had no hope of reaching.

Well, she could reach it if she scaled him like a climbing wall. Her eyes dropped to what would be a hell of a foothold before she got her bearings and put her hands on her hips.

"You know you're attractive." Betty cleared her throat. "Attractive enough to not bother with me when you made it big and took off around the world."

"You can't know how sorry I am that I left things the way I did." He handed her the picture back. "I thought you might have been keeping it for another reason. It's not every day I see a picture of myself stuck to my ex's fridge."

"Were we together long enough to call it a relationship? Don't worry about it, Nate. We were kids. Kids grow up, right?" She didn't have time to feel foolish when he pulled his lips between his teeth. She felt the burn she'd never lost for him start to smolder. She should be mad at herself, but all she could really feel was longing. Remembering the job that had taken him away before they'd had a chance to explore each other, she closed the gap between them. She had to ask: "What would have happened if you hadn't left?"

Nate's hand rested on her face. He tilted her chin up and suddenly Betty was back in school. She was performing on stage, and Nate was still her Romeo. Only he didn't have to leave for another country now. He was really here.

"I didn't want to leave. By the time they got me back in the states, you were already in college, and..."

She had tried to forget about Nate in college. She'd gone out on dates. But they'd never made her feel the butterflies she'd felt with Nate. No one had her laughing with joy as she read a letter. No one else sent her souvenirs of the world. Now Nate was here, and it should be awkward. Instead his hand touched her and she couldn't remember why she'd given up. He tucked a stray hair behind her ear and licked his lips. Her stomach fell out of her hoo-hah and flopped around at her feet like a fish out of water.

God, he was gorgeous.

But even with his stunning hazel eyes and adorable dimple, she realized she was keeping him from doing his job.

Betty coughed and stepped back. She ducked out of whatever spell he'd spun around her and waved her arm in the general direction of the sink. "I suppose I should let you get back to work. I promise, there will be no more pictures of yourself to distract you."

Well...there wouldn't be after she went to the bathroom and took the other one down.

This is a totally different type of buzz and woody...

Toy Story

April Fools For Love

There's nothing like hosting a pleasure toy party to broaden one's horizon. At least that's what Dana's experiencing every time she puts her products on the table and starts talking about them.

She's learning from her customers as much as they're learning from her. And when she gets the chance to put those lessons into practice? She goes for it, and discovers that she's a lot more inventive than she ever dreamed.

But Dana may be taking a huge risk, because not everyone is in favor of a good Toy Story.

Enjoy the following excerpt from *Toy Story*:

Dana finished her presentation and gave out a few door prizes and massage oil samples. The girls still giggled and chattered over the toys in the living room, so Dana went to the back bedroom to take orders and answer more personal questions.

One by one, they came and asked Dana about the toys, making their purchases in private. She was so happy they were pleased, and loved being able to explain away their worries with subtlety and non-judgmental words. Most had a preconceived notion that wanting to buy something like a fourteen-inch, double-ended, pulsating, rubber dildo was dirty and nasty. She listened and eased their fears, keeping mental notes of things to try when that topic arose.

Many of the women knew exactly what they wanted, either from a recommendation or because looking at it got them hot. She had sold seven vibrators, five clit massagers, a stress ball shaped like a pair of testicles, two pairs of handcuffs, a fluorescent yellow whip, three packages of pleasure creams and a partridge in a pear tree.

The last customer, Lisa, sat browsing through the catalog and pointed to a slender pink vibrator. "This looks nice."

"So what size would you like?" Dana asked the petite woman.

"Well, I'm not sure. I've never had one of these things. My husband is a computer salesman and leaves for weeks at a time, which is rough. Patty asked me to come to the party, and I figured this might curb the tension a little. What do you recommend?"

"What size are you used to?" Dana asked, trying to make her less nervous. "Here, look at this." Dana held up her hand, extending her middle three fingers.

"Is your husband this wide?" she asked holding up the three fingers.

"No, smaller than that." The woman blushed.

"What about this?" she asked again, holding up one finger.

"Noooo, wider than that."

Dana held her index and middle fingers up. She placed the fingers between her lips and sucked them into her mouth. "I'd say he's an average-sized man then. Hmm, let me think." Dana looked at Lisa and caught her nervous glance at the toys. Then she asked, "You ever hear of a 'Pocket Rocket'?"

Must Love Menage
© 2016 Kayleigh Malcolm

April Fools For Love

Chloe keeps a strict policy of not mixing work and play. But play is exactly what she wants with both her hotter than sin bosses.

Rumors and false accusations from an ex-girlfriend forced Ben and Sam to close their Florida restaurant and try to reopen one in Bayburgh. They've vowed to never date an employee again but the vivacious Chloe is temptation personified.

When a series of events cascades from a prank gone wrong, the three of them end up committed to running in a charity marathon. Training for the event throws them together outside of work and explore the attraction they've been fighting.

Will Ben and Sam to risk everything by inviting Chloe into their lives, not knowing if she's willing to be shared?

www.ingramcontent.com/pod-product-compliance
Lightning Source LLC
Chambersburg PA
CBHW060354180626
46817CB00008B/3003